Ghost Tales & Superstitions
of
Southern Appalachian Mountains

By:

Tammy J. Poore

Illustrations by:
Tammy J. Poore
and
Lavada J. Robbins

Nine Lives Publishing
Knoxville, TN

ISBN-13: 978-0-9844948-0-4
ISBN-10: 0-9844948-0-4

Dedicated to my loving husband,
our beautiful children,
and my wonderful Mom.

Contents

Acknowledgements.................... vi

Preface........................ viii

The Ghost of Big Rock.................. 1

A Late Eighteenth Century
Fortune Teller............................. 9

The Coughing Ghost.................... 15

The Legend of the
Missing Gloves........................... 25

The Ghosts of Dry Bones Ridge..... 35

Seven Mountain Boys...... 41

The Bones of Old Jim................... 49

The Haunting of Brush Arbor......... 61

Grandma Spirit............................ 75

Dead Man's Bones..................... 83

The Estate Sale.......................... 91

The Stansbury Legacy.................. 99

About The Author........................ 143

Acknowledgements:

I wish to say a special thanks to my Mother, for sharing these stories of the mountains, many of which happened during her childhood, some even before.

I wish to extend gratitude to my Aunt in Jacksboro,TN., for listening to the stories we've collected, and sharing her memories and thoughts.

I want to express gratitude to my husband and children, for giving me the space to write and the tools and encouragement to reach for my dream.

I also wish to thank friends and family in Tennessee, Ohio and North Carolina, for their encouraging words and also for believing in me.

I especially appreciate my relatives who are mentioned in this book, (their names changed of course to protect their identity).

I hope you will enjoy these ghost tales and superstitions as much as I have.

Ghost Tales & Superstitions
of
Southern Appalachian Mountains

Preface:

These short tales are a collection of unpublished stories, handed down from my wonderful mother.

The early chapters are based on tales which originated in the Appalachian Mountains of West Virginia & Tennessee, where my mother and her family lived when she was a child.

Understand that many of these narratives are from an era when there was no running water, no private restrooms, and no electricity. These stories have spanned nearly a century, and have been shared with many generations.

In earlier days gathering with neighbors, friends and family while sharing stories was very common and became almost a tradition. It was a grand way to pass the time.

Like similar ghost stories born from superstition, or stemming from mysterious events that defy rational explanation, each of these accounts include a ghost, a spiritual visitor or an element of the supernatural.

Though many traditional "ghost stories" were invented for the sole reason of scaring children away from dangerous locations, the stories in this book were never designed for that purpose.

The stories in this collection are based on truth, yet I realize that over the years much of the facts have been distorted, translated, or maybe a few details have even been added to the original story.

Isn't that the way a good ghost story begins?

Beliefs:

Are you afraid of ghosts?
There is no such thing as a ghost, so why would I be afraid?

What should I do if I see a ghost?
If you see a ghost, call it by name. This will evoke the ghost.

What if I don't know the ghost's name?
Shout at it and ask it to leave!

How can I keep spirits away?
Carry a vial of holy water.
Or carry a clove of garlic.
Or carry a vial of blessed Sea Salt.

What if the spirit visits me in my dreams?
Confuse the spirit by placing your shoes beneath your bed with one
shoe pointing in one direction and the other shoe pointing in the
opposite direction.

How can I protect my home from spirits?
Paint your door red, spirits won't enter through a red door.
Cover all mirrors in the house after someone dies, the ghost can't use
the mirror as a portal.

I've heard a ghost can't cross moving water.
Moving water represents life. A ghost is dead.

Well, then, if all these beliefs are true, why are there so many ghost
sightings?
I don't know, why don't you ask a ghost?

1

<u>The Ghost of Big Rock</u>

The Commissary was a place miners would gather in the evening to talk and share stories. Ghost stories were popular in those days and most had a basis of truth. The Ghost of Big Rock was a favorite to all who heard it.

Hugh explained one night a long time ago, the tale he was about to share happened before some of the men he was talking to was even born.

He had to make a trip down the mountain to the next settlement. When he came to the curve at the Big Rock, there standing beside of the road was a young girl, looking as though she was waiting for someone.

Her long black hair flowed in the wind and she wore a wreath of flowers around her head.

In the headlamps of Hugh's car it appeared as though her long white dress was damp as it clung to her slim body. As Hugh slowed his vehicle to a stop he could see that she was chilled as her body shivered and her skin was pale. She had a sad look about her.

Hugh said, "My first thought was that she was lost and she might be someone's daughter from the mountains. I stopped the car and reached over to open the passenger door. She got inside and I asked her where she was going at night by herself. She didn't say a word or even look my way. I told her I had to make a trip down to the next settlement and then I could take her back to her house if she lived in the mountains. She gave me a short nod. So we started on our way down the mountain."

At Big Rock there is a bad horseshoe curve and you have to keep your eyes on the narrow road or you could go off the bluff onto the tram track, or if you left the road in the right spot you might even go off into the waterfalls.

If you aren't familiar with Big Rock, you have to try to imagine it. It was a huge rock with a dirt road that ran down the mountain on the edge of a bluff with a waterfall flowing from the lower side of the mountain where a creek ran down the side as well. The road curved around the big rock in the shape of a horseshoe.

On one side of the rock the ground was flat and the grass stayed green all summer. Churches held outings there; young brides planned June weddings in the shade of this beautiful big rock. In the cool of the evening men would go there to relax and gamble in the shade.

When Hugh finally got past the sharp curve and the road straightened out, he relaxed and looked over to see how his passenger was doing, but no one was there.

"Did I imagine that I had seen a girl and picked her up in my car? I placed my hand over on the passenger seat and it was wet. For the record, it hadn't rained in days." Hugh knew his old T model Ford was not in good shape and parts of it were held together with wire. Could she have opened the door and jumped out while he was going around Big Rock without him noticing?

As he finished his journey to the settlement and back up the mountain again, Hugh could not get the sad little face of the young girl out of his mind, or the image of her frail body. He thought to himself that he might not want to tell anyone what had happened, they might think him crazy.

But all night long the face came back to him again and again as his mind replayed the events. He imagined her cold, pale body and wondered what could have happened to her.

The next day he could barely wait until work was over so he could go down to the Commissary to see if something had happened at The Big Rock.

As the men gathered around for their daily talk Hugh couldn't resist interrupting them of their idle chatter, "Fellows, you may think I'm crazy for asking, but did something happen to a girl at the Big Rock?"

Joe was older than Hugh and he spoke up first, "Oh, you must have met the ghost of Big Rock?"

The validation that there was indeed something tangible relieved Hugh and he nodded, eagerly awaiting the story.

"She was a very young girl," Joe continued, "Let me tell you the story my father told me long ago right here at this old commissary. This young girl, Betty Anne, planned her wedding in June when the wild flowers would be in bloom. Her father Henry brought bales of hay for family and friends to sit on. Betty Anne had picked wild flowers and arranged them around a stage her father had built for her. Her mother Dot had made a fancy wedding cake and the family carried down a bucket of fresh spring water.

"There was Bud, her boy friend she loved very much and looked forward to marrying. Jane was her maid of honor. She had grown up with this girl and they were like sisters. The two girls had been together all day decorating and getting everything in proper order. Betty Anne was humming happily to herself as she worked, her family noticed.

"It was almost time for the rest of the family and friends to show up for the big event, so Betty Anne stepped behind some bushes to slip into her white wedding dress. She placed a wreath of wild flowers around her head and stepped out from behind the bushes to show Bud and Jane. But, you see, they didn't see her, they were too busy embraced in each other's arms, kissing. Betty Anne ran out from around the big rock crying, and after that she disappeared.

"Henry and Dot didn't see their daughter run away, but when they started asking questions about where their daughter was, Jane told them she had gone for a walk around the horse shoe curve. This puzzled the parents, as they knew she wouldn't go without Bud. Why would she go for a walk by herself when it was time for her wedding?

"Dot and Henry went to look for themselves. When they came to the bluff and looked over the edge, they didn't see anything. They were relieved; at least she hadn't fallen from the bluff. They also walked on down to the tram track, still no sign of Betty Anne. Then they went down to the water falls.

"There, lying on a slick flat rock was their beautiful daughter with the wreath of wild flowers still in her hair, and her long, white dress flowing gently in the water.

"Had she fallen on the slick rock and hit her head? Was it possible something more sinister had happened taking the life of Betty Anne?

"Later, it turned out that Bud and Jane admitted they had been caught kissing. They admitted that saw Betty Anne running away, crying. But they claim they didn't know anything else.

"The parents realized that if this story was true, why hadn't Bud or Jane went to check on her? Why had they lied when first asked about Betty Anne's where-abouts?" It was then that Joe paused for a long while, and then he picked up the story, "There wasn't any way to know for sure what did happen since Bud and Jane kept to their stories all their lives. But many say the reason that the ghost of Big Rock walks around on certain nights is that she is waiting for someone to find out what really happened. I reckon the ghost will walk that road for as long as the road is here, because Bud and Jane took the truth with them to their graves."

Before Hugh could grasp the story that had been told, another man named Mel spoke up then, "So you saw her for yourself, then, Hugh?"

Hugh admitted, "I gave her a ride in my car."

Mel nodded solemnly, "Though many have seen her, none of us have. We've just heard the story passed down through the years. Some say she won't speak. Some say she points over to the spot where her wedding was to be."

Hugh wondered if she had pointed to the clearing at Big Rock. He hadn't looked over at her once he started driving until he hit the straight away, "She didn't speak to me." He said.

"Just as well," Mel stated in a deep, somber voice. He dropped his chin and lifted his eyes just as Hugh looked his way, "They say that if she does speak, the driver will surely die. Many have, at least that's what I've always heard."

That's when Hugh decided he had heard enough. He got up from his seated position and thanked the men for their story and got into his T model Ford. He looked over at the seat where the night before a ghost had rode alongside, and he gave a silent nod of thanks that he never did hear her speak.

Since time began humans have longed to know what the future holds for them. Psychics and Fortune Tellers have always been here. They are even mentioned in the Bible. It is little wonder the God fearing people of the mountains were fascinated, mystified and feared those who claim to know the future.
As told by my mother.

2

A Late Eighteenth Century Fortune Teller

Aunt Hazel, thinking of her brings a mixture of emotions. She was a fascinating woman. She was charming and attractive, a real delight to be around. She could easily draw you into her captivating ways.

It was the ease in which she captivated people that caused our Daddy to warn his children when she came to visit, "Don't let Aunt Hazel tell your fortune." He would say. He knew that children were easily influenced.

People in the mountains would walk miles to have her read their fortune when she visited West Virginia.

Aunt Hazel particularly fascinated the young children the most. They would become spell bound as she told the future with an air of mystery surrounding her strange mannerisms.

The excitement she brought to our house when she visited was comparable to a holiday. My sisters and I sat in awe, watching her brush her long, thick hair at night before turning in for bed; the way she twisted one thick braid down her back seemed almost magical, as it looked like a thick, black snake when she was done.

Hazel was very superstitious and it was widely known she didn't trust anyone. Maybe that's because she could see the inner side of most folk. As a result of her mistrust, she wore an Ace bandage on her beautiful legs to hide money; knowing that few people were brave enough to undertake stealing from her she would dutifully tuck the bills away in the folds of the bandage. It was feared she would put a hex on anyone who crossed her. No one would dare take that chance.

If you were lucky enough to be her friend, she would do anything for you. It was clear she felt that way about Joan, her best friend. Aunt Hazel lived a state away, yet she always made time to visit Joan, staying a week or two, spending as much time with her as she could.

Joan had eight children and one on the way at the time of this story. Seth was Joan's husband. He worked on the railroad and was a strong young man who had to make a good living to raise a big family.

Seth and Aunt Hazel had a deep discord for one another. Was he jealous because Hazel cared more for his wife? Or, did he fear Hazel? Was there something else that had happened? Perhaps something Hazel had detected that made Seth uncomfortable in her presence. Whatever the answer, it went with them to their graves.

Seth's wife, Joan, was much younger than he was, and not strong enough to have one baby right after the other. Ole Dr. Will had warned Seth about the danger of having more babies after the eighth child was born. He said, "Seth, I am afraid Joan will die during childbirth if she gets in the family way again."

Joan indeed became weaker with each baby born, once a strong woman in her youth, Joan's appearance was becoming ragged and frail for her years.

Aunt Hazel knew about Joan's health, as friends often share these kinds of details. During the pregnancy of the ninth child Hazel visited more often to help with cooking, washing clothes, caring for the other children, anything she could do to assist the family. Aunt Hazel didn't ask for any money, it was a friend helping a friend.

As the due date approached Joan went into labor a few weeks early. It was a long and difficult birth with a lot of blood lost. Though the baby seemed healthy, Joan was pale and lethargic, unable to awaken fully after the baby was born. Joan died the next morning after giving birth to her last child.

Naturally Aunt Hazel was hurt, and saddened that nine little children had lost a mother. Not only sad, Hazel was mad at Seth who had been selfish, continually impregnating his wife even after the doctor had warned him.

Aunt Hazel was known to speak her mind, and this time she didn't want any mistake made about what she said, "Seth, you listen and you listen well," She told him, "Every pain your wife ever suffered in child birth you will suffer before you die!"

After the funeral Aunt Hazel went back to her home in Kentucky. She didn't return to visit or look in on Seth. Her discord for him was so deep that she would ask friends and neighbors about the children, but never asked about him.

As for Seth, within a month of the funeral he took to his bed. Dr. Will made house calls to see him but couldn't find anything wrong.

Seth said he was in pain and couldn't walk. He could find little comfort, nor any strength to perform daily routines.

About six months after Joan's death Seth sent for my Daddy.

Seth asked, "You know your sister has put a hex on me, and I will not get any better until she comes down here and takes it off. Will you go to Kentucky and bring her back to remove the spell?"

Daddy answered, "Seth, Hazel can't put anything on you, it's all in your mind. But if nothing else will help you, I will ask her to come back here." Though our Daddy didn't believe she could put a curse on anyone, he would do his part to help.

Seth had every reason to believe Aunt Hazel could put a curse on someone. She was well known in three states, even requested by local authorities who would turn to her for help in solving missing person cases on occasion.

One time a young girl was missing and the authorities had reason to believe she might have been murdered. They had already searched for months with no clue as to her whereabouts. They visited Hazel to ask for her assistance.

Hazel could put herself into some sort of trance and claimed to see things in this state of mind, so she agreed to help the detectives. She told them the girl they sought was dead, and she told them where to find the body. They found the child's body exactly where Hazel said it would be. This seemed to bring a certain amount of local fame to Hazel, fame that she did not seek, nor want.

It was enough proof for many, including Seth, that she was indeed a real fortune teller.

Even though Daddy convinced Hazel to come back to West Virginia to tell Seth she hadn't put a hex on him, her words didn't make a difference, as he died a little over a year later.

The doctor was never able to name an illness, but indeed something went wrong, as Seth had unbearable pain and couldn't walk by himself soon after he took to his bed.

Could it have been the power of suggestion that made him believe he was in pain? If so, could that same power of suggestion have actually led to his death? Or, did Aunt Hazel really have the power to put a hex on him? To this day no one really knows.

3

<u>The Coughing Ghost</u>

One of my favorite ghost stories was handed down from my grandfather, who was deceased years before my birth. The story has survived decades, and even though I have heard it many times since my childhood, very little has been added to, or taken away from the original tale. It is based on truth, as it actually happened to my grandfather Jim.

My grandfather was a coal miner, as were most of the men of his era. He moved to coal mining camps wherever work was available. During this particular time of his life he had journeyed to a coal mining camp in Rich Mountain, West Virginia, in search of a job and housing for his family.

He spoke with a foreman and was told, "Jim, we've got plenty of work for ya, but we've only got one house available and I might as well tell ya, not many men want to live in it."

"That won't be a problem, I'm handy with the tools, and I can fix it up."

The foreman paused and looked at Jim, who stood over six feet tall with broad shoulders, and was a solid, upright man for his age, "Jim, I believe you could fix the old house up just fine. But that ain't what I'm talkin' about." The foreman then lowered his voice, stepping closer to speak, "That ole house is haunted. Not many men

15

can stay there very long, and you have them children to think about."

My grandfather was a respectful man, and he was a religious man. He believed in the good Lord and his faith was strong. He wouldn't offend the man by scoffing at a ghost tale, especially since he was being offered work and a

house in the coal mining camp for his family. After a respectful moment of thought he said, "I'll take that house, even if it's haunted. If there is a ghost, I'll catch it."

Of course my grandfather did right by his wife and children; he told them the ghost story, reminding that there was a rational explanation since he had never met a ghost yet. But if there was one he promised he would catch it.

He explained that so far no one had ever seen the phantom, it had been heard hobbling throughout the house, coughing, shuffling like an old man walking with a cane.

Like any excitable child his youngest daughter looked forward to hearing the ghost walk through the house. Not that anyone in his family was actually afraid, mind you. But they had never lived in a real haunted house before.

The family busily started making a home out of the old house. Each person had a fair share of chores to do, including the children, as was the custom in those days.

Jim did his part of fixing the windows, repairing the tin roof, getting the house up to par after it had sat empty and neglected for some time.

It wasn't immediate that the ghost made its first appearance, but it did happen, just as the legend foretold.

Long after the family had settled into bed one night, the sounds of thumps and bumps brought the family fully awake.

The distant sound of slow, shuffling footsteps, followed by the solid thump of a cane hitting the floor from afar amplified in the eerie darkness.

Jim lit an oil lamp to further investigate the unknown visitor. The shuffling noise and the thump continued: Scuffle... thump...cough. Scuffle...thump... followed by the wheezy cough of an old smoker.

Jim pursued the noise with his three children close behind him, each holding the shirt tale of the one in front of them.

Even with the remnants of a fire in the fireplace, and the glow from the oil lamp, there were darkened corners of the room, places behind furniture that could easily conceal a figure in the shadows.

Shadows that seemed to dance slowly, moving from side to side, catching the eye of each family member as they looked for the ghostly spirit which had aroused them from their sleep.

The youngest daughter whimpered softly when the ghost coughed very nearby, it sounded from just behind them. Everyone turned to look in the same direction, Jim holding the lamp out at arm's length.

No movements, no shadows, no ghost.

Only silence.

No cough, no thump, no shuffle.

Each family member strained their eyes for any ghostly shape or figure. But there seemed to be nothing, or no one in the room other than them.

By now the mother had illuminated another lantern and entered the room, which brought much relief to the children because instantly the room was brightened and the shadows weren't nearly as foreboding.

"Jim, come to bed. Come now, children." She suggested after scanning the room, "There is no such thing as ghosts."

"Your mother is right, children, back to bed." He placed a comforting hand on the shoulder of his oldest daughter, "In the morning I'll check it out. I'm sure there's a reason for the noises. See, there is no ghost in here." He swept the lantern outward and showed the room was indeed absent of a ghost.

The family returned to their beds. Though sleep didn't come readily, it did finally come and by morning the fear of the ghost was pushed to the backs of their minds. In the absence of darkness the house didn't look as frightening as it had the night before.

True to his word, Jim investigated the fireplace and checked the stone hearth for cracks or holes. He looked at the rocking chair, rocking it back and forth, seeking an explanation for the noises they had all heard the night before. When he studied the wood walls he rubbed his palms over a few small cracks, "These need fixin', a good gust of wind would whistle right through here."

That evening he busied himself patching holes and filling in the cracks between the slats of wood.

That night there wasn't a ghostly visitor. Nor the night after that.

In fact, it might have been another week before Jim heard the intruding noise again. This time he heard the scuffle first, before he had even drifted off to sleep.

The children did not stir. He eased up in bed and turned his good ear toward the sound. The noise sounded like an old man unable to lift his feet much, shuffling them across the floor.

Jim draped his legs over the edge of the bed and sat upright, trying not to make much noise as he didn't want to disturb his wife, or their children resting nearby.

The sound was coming from the kitchen.

Scuffle, shuffle, thump…

The old ghost must have been winded because he paused for a few minutes, then wheezed and coughed.

The noise brought one of the children awake, "Daddy!" She softly cried out.

"Shhh!" Jim pointed a finger up, "Let your ole Pa catch the ghost this time." He whispered.

He quietly lifted the glass globe from the lantern and struck a match. The scrape of the match startled the old ghost for a moment or two, because again all became silent.

Jim waited patiently. He didn't move. His outstretched arm and finger keeping his excited daughter quiet, too.

The flame from the lantern settled down to a calm flicker as Jim adjusted the length of the wick. He eased up to his full height.

From the kitchen he heard a couple of bumps, but the old ghost wasn't walking. It did cough though, and Jim trod as quietly as he could, taking soft steps each time the old man coughed, this covered the sounds of Jim's footsteps.

Taking a few steps, then pausing to wait, Jim was determined he would catch the noise-maker this night. No matter how long it took.

Then the shuffling sound started and it seemed to be going away from Jim. Scuffle, thump, cough. Scuffle, a thump from the cane, and then cough.

Jim lifted his lantern when he got to the kitchen, visibly jumping at the sight of a dark, slouching shadow moving directly in front of his eyes.

Poor old man had a hunch back.

Jim stopped moving. His daughter could see him standing there, looking hard in the direction of something… then he motioned with his hand for her to come near.

The little girl's heart was pounding fast: What had her daddy caught? Was she really going to see a genuine ghost?

She tiptoed towards her father, hoping she would get there in time to see the ghost before it vanished.

The room had become quiet for the most part; she could only hear the sound of her light footsteps and her heart beating inside her ears.

She eased up behind her father, leaning around to see; She almost squealed when saw the dark figure. But Jim had already put his arm around her shoulder and was drawing her out from behind him, whispering, "Shhh, he doesn't know we're here. Look in the corner."

The child looked and saw the ghost this time, not just his shadow.

Jim said, "Told you we'd catch a ghost. Let's not wake anyone, we'll have a story to tell in the morning."

By now their presence was known to the nightly intruder and the shadow was moving away into the dark corners of the room. Jim and his daughter were too excited about seeing their ghostly visitor to know where it went after it became concealed in the darkness.

By morning they could hardly wait to tell the rest of the family about it.

Sitting around the table, the daughter eagerly piped up. "We caught the ghost last night! Me and Daddy really saw it!"

The remaining children exchanged disbelieving looks and the mother put her fork down, asking, "Jim, is this true?"

"Sure is." He said, "I heard it shuffling around in the kitchen. When I got there I saw the humped over shadow on the wall. But that was the shadow caused from the light in the lamp; the ghost was in the corner. He was pretty old, and in bad shape."

All the children sat upright, they couldn't believe what their father was telling them.

"I thought there was no such thing as a ghost?" The oldest daughter challenged, looking between her mother and her father for an explanation.

"That's his name, ain't it?" Jim chuckled, "We've been looking for a ghost, and last night we caught it."

"Was it a real ghost, Daddy?" The youngest one chimed in.

"Nah!" Jim laughed, "It was an old rat. Gone nearly blind and had lost a foot to a trap. He was a big one, though, probably as big as a cat." Jim put his foot down, scooting it across the floor, "The shuffling noises came from his tail dragging across the floor, and the thump we thought was a cane was the old rat putting that stub leg down."

"What about the cough?" A daughter asked.

Jim mimicked a gruff, coughing sound, "The old rat wheezes and coughs, his breathing is not so good."

"He was eating food crumbs." The daughter who had helped find the ghost explained, "He was right over there in that corner." She pointed. Bursting out laughing as all eyes turned to where the ole rat had been.

No one ever told the foreman or any of the neighbors about the identity of the mysterious ghost. Whenever it was mentioned, Jim would say, "Aww, we don't believe in ghosts. But if there is one, I'll catch it."

4

The Legend of the Missing Gloves

As told by my mother:

When my family lived in Rich Mountain, our school house also served as a church and a gathering place for many special functions, including annual pie suppers.

The building consisted of one big room with a "pot belly" stove in the middle of the room.

The coal mining company owned the building and also paid for a teacher to come in and teach all of the grades, which at that time was 1st-8th.

At the annual pie suppers we had cake walks, bobbing for apples, and plenty of different home baked, delicious pies; it was always a lot of fun for children as well as adults.

Often there were a few bullies who especially liked to tease girls and pick on the smaller boys.

In particular there was this girl we went to school with who the bullies liked to torment; her name was Kate.

She was unusually shy and didn't talk much. The bullies, John and Wally, liked to poke fun at Kate and play mean little tricks on her.

We were always told that she was "tongue tied", she had a speech defect. Our Daddy told us to be kind to her, that the reason she was shy might be because she was ashamed of her speech impediment.

Kate would stand off from the children at school during recess, and even at the pie suppers and church gatherings. She would not join in any of the games or festivities. When she did try to join in the games the meaner children would push her down and laugh at her.

Kate was friendly with the children who were nice to her, and she could be a lot of fun if you gave her a chance. Even though she wasn't easy to understand when she spoke, we tried to be friendly to her.

She was a clean girl and also kind of pretty. But that didn't stop some of the children from mistreating her.

In the mountains everyone took responsibility for their belongings. In the winter we had our coat and gloves to take care of, and we were all very careful with them because it was all we got to last through the long, cold winter season.

What happened to Kate at the pie supper should never happen to anyone, least of all her.

It was a typical gathering with children playing games and adults talking and preparing for the pie supper.

No one noticed that Kate was missing, neither the teacher or the parents or the children. We were not aware of how long she had been missing, not until after the pie supper was over and clean up preparations had begun.

It was one of the parents who started asking about Kate. Word quickly traveled through the group with everyone asking, "Have you seen Kate?"

Inside the building people would hang their coats on large nails on the wall, and someone noticed that Kate's coat was still hanging on the nail, but that her gloves were missing.

This seemed very odd, for why would she go outside without her coat yet take her gloves? The other oddity was that for girls coats, the gloves were on a long string threaded through the inside from arm to arm, and stitched to the collar so the gloves couldn't be lost.

Why had she removed her gloves from the coat at all? This caused alarm and everyone began searching for Kate.

We separated into small groups and started calling out her name, hoping she would answer. We all hoped she was hiding, maybe hiding from the bullies who always picked on her, pulling their pranks and being downright mischievous with rough horseplay and unkind words.

Everyone searched for a long time, some even walked to her parents' home to see if she had gone home alone.

Since winter nights in the mountains were bitter cold, in the back of our minds we all knew that if Kate wasn't found that night, her chances of being found alive were slim.

Long up in the early morning hours after the children were put to bed only a few remaining men and women searched with lanterns. The adults decided to take a break and get warm. They needed to change into dry clothing and rest awhile before starting the search anew at the break of dawn.

Their hearts were heavy, for they knew that without a miracle, the morning would start with them searching for a body instead of a girl child.

Morning came and the adults began the search above the school house, walking into the woods, then around the top of the ridge of the mountain with no luck at all.

The women stayed closer to the school house. One woman left the group to use the outhouse near the school.

Now, no one can say what happened to Kate, but when the men and women heard Mrs. Long cry out and holler up towards the mountain to "Hurry down to the girls' toilet!" because she had found something, the men and women quickly responded.

When they arrived at the outhouse, Mrs. Long opened the door and asked one man to look inside, "Look down the end hole on the left." She instructed.

The girls outside toilet had four holes set over a dipper ditch. There, on a dirt ledge about three feet down was Kate's little gloves, string still attached.

Finding the gloves only raised more questions. Had Kate gone out all alone the night before to use the toilet? Had she dropped her gloves down the hole and tried to reach them and fallen into the mire?

It seemed unlikely that she had gone to the outhouse on a cold, dark night alone, especially without a light. Still, there were her gloves. But where was Kate?

The adults knew what they had to do. They would have to tear down the old outhouse and dig through the mire and waste. It was a painstaking task, and they feared they would find the body of the little girl.

All day the men labored, until sunset, and there still wasn't a body or any sign of Kate. Finally, after much frustration, the group decided to stop digging through the mire. They realized they had lost valuable time. Instead of continuing the search of the mountain they had spent the day searching through human waste in the toilet hole after finding Kate's gloves on the dirt ledge in the outhouse.

A few of the men grumbled that maybe it had been a mischievous prank , the boys could have took Kate's gloves and tossed them down the toilet hole, maybe Kate had never gone to the outhouse at all.

After three days of looking for Kate, the search party was called off. It was a sad realization that either Kate had been lured away, or had ran away. Or maybe the reason the gloves were in the toilet was because the bullies pulled a cruel joke that turned deadly wrong after Kate had followed them outside to get her gloves back, and they tried to hide the evidence. The questions remained unanswered.

Sometimes it seems children can be the cruelest of all. The bullies continued their pranks on the school grounds during recess, taunting the smaller children to tears. It never appeared to bother them that Kate went missing and was never found.

The next year at the annual pie supper the events went on as they always had. Except on this day, someone noticed something a little different. On the nail where Kate had hung her coat the year before, there was the same brown coat she had worn. This created much talk, as you can imagine, since the coat had not been there since the day she went missing.

Word quickly spread through the crowd that someone had hung Kate's coat on the nail as a cruel prank.

Then later, when the pie supper was nearing the end, the children became excited, started pointing and talking and whispering about something they saw.

They had seen a familiar little girl reaching up to get her coat. They said it was Kate who had returned from the beyond. When a few adults went to see what the burst of excitement was about, the little girl and the brown coat simply vanished.

Even though the vision was shared by many who attended the supper that night, and there was much talk for weeks after the pie supper, the bullies seemed undaunted. They continued their practice of teasing and taunting smaller children.

Two years after Kate went missing there were still no answers as to her whereabouts and no one knew what had happened to her. It was the night of the pie supper again, and the nail where Kate had hung her coat was empty.

This was something the children were anxious to see, because they had eagerly awaited the second anniversary of her disappearance to see if the same thing would happen, if Kate would return to claim her coat.

Even though the nail was empty, little did we know we were in for a strange surprise.

During the evening, John and Wally went outside to the boys outhouse to use the toilet.

John was standing outside to hold the door. Suddenly he heard Wally talking to someone.

John asked him, "Who are you talking to?"

Wally didn't answer him. He had become silent.

John tried to open the door after Wally didn't answer, but a strange gurgling sound came from inside the outhouse. It was a sound he had never heard before. It was a very eerie noise.

John ran as fast as he could back to the school house to get help, he knew something was wrong with his friend.

Parents and teachers took their lanterns, following him to the outside toilets.

The door came open with ease this time when one of the men tried it. There, cowering in the corner was Wally. His face pale and his eyes wide, you could see by his expression that he had seen something that frightened him.

Two men attempted to help Wally up, but he started shaking his head in resistance from side to side.

Someone asked him what was wrong. When he tried to answer, no one could understand him. He was tongue tied.

Had Kate come back and named her murderer? It seemed so. Because when the teacher and the parents returned to the school house, there, hanging on Kate's nail was her dirty pair of gloves, with string still intact.

Had someone planted the gloves there to get a confession? Or was it Kate herself, back from beyond, who came to seek justice? No one can say for sure, as Kate's body was never found.

Kate's nail remained empty in the old school house for many years; no one used the nail to hang coats on, as it was known as Kate's nail.

Much to the disappointment of the children, her coat or gloves were never seen on the nail again, even at the annual pie supper.

As for Wally, he never spoke plain so no one ever knew what he saw in the outhouse that night. But you can safely say that whatever he encountered changed his life forever. Wally nor John had an interest in being bullies anymore. In fact, Wally became very shy, withdrawing from even his friends.

The other bullies grew older and were replaced with newer bullies, as there will always be a few mischief makers in every crowd, but the taunting was never as malicious as what Kate had endured.

Could it have been because each year at the annual pie supper, the mysterious story of Kate's gloves was repeated for generations to come?

5

The Ghosts of Dry Bones Ridge

I always loved to hear my mother speak of "Dry Bones Ridge." The name alone suggested spooky images of skeletal remains and promises of fright.

When my mother was growing up, the children were expected to help the parents with household chores. Their day to day lives involved working as much if not more than playing. But children often make their chores a little more entertaining, and this may have a lot to do with the wonderful tale of Dry Bones Ridge.

To reach the gap of the mountain from where my mother's family lived, they had to go through Dry Bones Ridge. The "gap" is where the two mountains met, and a wagon road ran through the base of the mountains.

When the cows were dry, or the hens didn't lay, my grandmother, Bea, would send my mom and her older sister to Pap and Granny's house on the other side of the mountain for the supplies they needed.

Even at noon, when the sun was high in the sky, very little of the natural light penetrated the thick overgrowth of trees, shrubs, and bushes; producing a cool, dusky feel during the day. Thick moss covered the rocks and much of the ground where grass couldn't grow.

My mother's interpretation of traveling the wagon road through Dry Bones Ridge.

There seemed to always be eyes watching the two little travelers from the dense trees. My mother and her sister would tread carefully, clutching hands as they went on their way.

The breeze carried unknown voices, saying, "You can't run, you can't hide, for my eyes see you all the time."

This would send shivers and goose bumps all over the children, causing their hearts to race from fear.

On both sides of the wagon road from the mysterious darkness surrounding them, hundreds of bright red, blinking eyes followed the young girls.

The faster they walked, or even if they ran, the eyes would follow them, getting closer and closer, until the girls could feel the cold stare of the ghosts, and something unfathomable barely touching their skin just as they would dart away.

The older girl often told her younger sister, "Climb onto my back and I will run as fast as I can!"

The relief that flooded their scared little souls left them breathless when they safely emerged from the wooded ridge. But the knowledge that they had to go back the same way they had traveled, while carrying their supplies back home worried them even more. The fear weighed heavily on them before every trip.

My mom and her sister had heard many tales about Dry Bones Ridge, especially from their uncle who told about what he had seen on that ridge, and how it scared him so bad that his hair stood up on his head. He'd tell the girls, "If there was any other way to the gap, I would not be found dead up there in Dry Bones Ridge."

When he spoke of the spirits of all the dead, with the hundreds of glowing, red eyes, watching weary travelers, hearing the haunting voices carrying on the wind, it made the children's hearts beat louder and faster, because they knew what it was like, they had heard the voices and seen those eyes, they had felt the same fear as their uncle. He was a grown man, and he didn't like to travel through the gap.

He mentioned running from the spirits, after finding the dried bones of the lost and weary scattered throughout the woods. Skulls and femur bones, some in a pile, others strewn about. Empty eye sockets turned upwards in the skulls with vacant stares; but the only eyes watching those who traveled through the Ridge were the eyes from the angry spirits, glowing menacingly from the darkness.

The families in the mountains would go to stir offs where some of the adults made sorghum molasses. Children and adults alike loved to share scary stories, especially about the "Ghosts of Dry Bones Ridge".

The tale was that over many years there were dozens of people lost in those mountains, never to be found.

Children, young people and even old people had become disoriented and couldn't find their way through the dense overgrowth. Some of the lost unfortunate people died from the bitter cold winters. Others were killed by wild animals, wolves or even bear; the only remains found were the bones of the missing.

Oh, but the scariest tales were rumors of innocent people being ravaged by the angry ghosts, just as the ridge promised, "You can't run, you can't hide, for my eyes see you all the time."

In the imagination of many innocent children, even the moss became something to fear. It was often slippery from the dampness of the woods, and could easily cause a person to fall, then it could quickly gobble them up, never to be seen alive again, leaving just their bones behind!

My Mom said that she and her sister learned how to get through the gap of the mountain back from Pap's and Granny's house. They would run fast down the wagon road from their home, outrunning the voices because they didn't have to carry a sack full of supplies. But on the way back up, they had to carry eggs, bread and milk. They couldn't afford to drop and break the precious goods, so they would sing songs to the tops of their lungs, to drown out the haunting voices.

But there was no escaping the eyes, those bright, glowing, red eyes, following them all the way... always getting closer and closer.

6

<u>Seven Mountain Boys</u>

Along with the natural beauty of the mountains, there are many mysteries embedded in the valleys, and high atop the peaks. Mysteries that defy reason, that remain unsolved. Morals and values were important for mountain families, and children grew up respecting the big mountain where they lived. Taught from a very early age, the children of the mountains knew the dangers, yet sometimes tragedies found their way into the coal mining communities none the less.

My mother told me about a mystery that occurred when she was a child herself. To this day, no one has conclusive answers as to what happened that fateful weekend long ago.

We lived in the valley at the foot of the mountain where we knew everyone. We did not fear each other, and we did not fear the mountain, we respected it.

As children we roamed and played in the mountains, swinging on grape vines, swimming in little creeks, climbing trees, wading in mud puddles. Parents didn't worry about children playing in the woods all day. Not until the fateful day when seven boys went for a weekend campout up to the peak of the mountain.

Boys had always camped out and stayed overnight to hunt or fish, no one thought anything about it. It seemed as safe as being in your own backyard.

But when Sunday night came and none of the boys had returned home their parents became worried, wondering what might have happened to them.

Questions were asked aloud, "Did one of the boys fall and the others had to carry my boy off the mountain hurt?"

Other parents were more hopeful, thinking the youth had lost track of time, praying that the boys would arrive later in the night.

Little did they know the tragedy that awaited them on the peak of the mountain, nor how it would change their lives forever.

Sunday night went by with prayers and tears, and hope for the boys to come home safe. When morning came, and still there was no sign of them, they knew the young people were lost, so the men organized a group to search for them.

That Monday morning at daybreak a large group of men left for the peak of the mountain, which was an all day hike, even for the strongest of men.

There was no way the men could have prepared for the ghastly sight that awaited them. When they finally reached the peak, what they saw haunted them the rest of their lives.

The horrible sight before them was so shocking and gruesome, not one man in the group had ever seen anything like it.

My mother's interpretation of how the boys were found.

There, in a perfect circle lay seven bodies on the ground. Everything around the bodies was trampled down; even the sapling trees were bent and broken. Whatever had happened up there on the peak, even the earth had taken a beating.

The boys had each been beaten to death, their shirts torn and blood stained, their faces rigid masks of horror. It was their faces, the men later explained, and their eyes, forever etched in the memories of fathers and uncles who discovered them that haunted the grown men.

Who or **what** could have done this? Exactly **when** had it happened? No one knew how long they had been dead, but the stench of death was already tainting the air.

The task was for the men to get the boys' bodies off the mountain. All the vultures and scavenger animals would be moving in to feast on the decaying flesh; they were surprised they hadn't already.

43

The men hurriedly made sleds using two long poles for the sides and short ones across the center to pull the bodies off the mountain.

When they came back down into the valley of the mountain, people came in droves realizing the news was bad since the men were pulling a couple of sleds, and the sight of a mound of bodies heaped atop one another brought tears of pain, and wails of horror.

Mothers covered the smaller children's eyes, and some women fainted. People asked **what** had happened, and **why**, and **who** would do such a horrible thing?

Seven graves had to be dug. The boys had to be buried soon; the smell of death was worsening.

The pain of a terrible loss was overwhelming. The fear of **what**, or **who** could have done this unspeakable horror haunted all who knew of it. There was no rest for the families that night. No peace. Only pain, only questions.

Never had anything claimed the lives of as many young in such a tragic and frightening manner.

Down through the years, people pondered if it had been the revenuers looking for moonshine steels, inadvertently discovering the seven boys, and deciding for whatever reason to kill them.

Or maybe the reverse took place and the boys had innocently come upon a moonshine steel and were killed for their discovery.

Many of the men returned to the spot where the earth had withered a beating and the lives of seven youth were pummeled to death. They had probed around the area, each one taking his time and searching high and low, never finding a nearby steel or even parts of one. Never finding so much as a clue.

Some folk speculated that the boys had gone atop the mountain to commit a self-murder by fighting each other to the very death. Others thought there might have been a gang of unknowns who came into the mountains and caught the youth away from their homes, beating them so horribly and brutally that most were not recognized by their faces, but by the clothing they wore.

Yet the real mystery was why were the bodies all strewn around in a circular fashion? Why were the saplings, bushes and tall grass beaten to the ground, too, making the outline of a ring surrounding the seven boys?

Years later, even speculation of a space ship was mentioned. This mystery became the focus at local gatherings for many years. The questions plagued all of the families living in the mountains during that time, as it seemed that each resident had been robbed of their comfort, robbed of innocence, robbed of peace.

One question spawned another question. If the boys had come upon fearful people, why hadn't one or more ran for help? If it had been outsiders, how could a few boys or even grown men overtake seven healthy mountain boys?

How could a small area confine such a brawl to a circular pattern and even break the small trees from the force of the rampage?

So many questions, yet there seemed to be only theories instead of answers. The clues were few. There had not been a camp fire; the boys hadn't even put out their bed rolls.

All that the families knew was that they had tragically lost their sons that weekend. It not only hurt the boys' mothers and fathers, it hurt all who lived in the mountains and knew of it.

As years passed, time did not forget the unmerciful way that seven lives were taken from the innocent youth, or the heartache suffered by their families and friends.

Many children and their parents would look up towards that mountain peak, especially at night, when stars twinkled and lights flickered from unknown sources in the woods, thinking of the seven boys. Wondering if life would return to normal and if trust would embed itself in the mountain tradition once more, where children could play without fear.

Only the heavens knew the truth as to what had happened. But to this day, on certain nights, many still hear blood curdling screams and cries coming from that part of the woods, a sound so hauntingly eerie that the listener feels a chill and is covered with goose flesh.

It isn't too difficult to find the area where it happened, even now. The saplings that were bent to the ground and survived now grow tall, though somewhat twisted, and the earth around those trees seem to have a circular pattern where the grass is a different shade of green and always seems to blow in one direction.

———————————————————

In Rich Mountain
by
Lavada Robbins (C) 1991

In Rich Mountain a whistle blows,
Death has visited the mine below.
Women, children and old men, too,
Wait in fear, they know not who.

Prayers go up to the Lord above,
Please don't let it be the one I love.
Guilt riddled hearts, they look around,
Wives, sweethearts, mothers with young sons.

Death has taken someone today,
From the cold dark pit where they lay.
Hearts will be broken for all around,
Still, the miners must work underground.

Please, Dear Lord, answer our prayers today,
Keep them safe, out of harm's way.
Working the mine is all they know,
To raise a family in the mountains here.

7

The Bones of Old Jim

As told by my mother:

"Old Jim" had more questions than answers. No one knew how long he had been waiting in a hollow room, under the ground in a coal mine.

If it had not been for World War Two, he might still be there waiting. The old mine shafts Number One and Two had been sealed off for years.

I often heard my Daddy talk about finding Old Jim. We wondered aloud when Old Jim was waiting for rescue, had he thought about his family? Had he prayed for someone to find him? Being sealed in the mining room, knowing there was just hours left to live, had his mind gone back in time to when he was little boy? Or had he thought about when he was a young man on his first date? If he had been a father, had he spent his last living hours remembering the birth of his children?

Daddy explained that by the way Old Jim was found sitting on the ledge with his arm resting on a piece of coal, it was clear he had lived for a while after the rock slide.

Daddy and some more men had been contracted to strip iron track, and any other iron from the old mines for the defense department when World War Two began.

Daddy explained that the workers started stripping the iron at the mouth of the mine, removing iron tracks before working their way into any rooms. When they finally did come upon the room where Old Jim was, they had to break through the sealed shaft where long ago there had been a slate slide. The men labored long and hard before breaking through the slate rock into room number two. The instant the air entered the room they all saw a miner sitting on a ledge, and then the next moment it was nothing but a pile of bones.

The workers talked it over and thought it would be cruel to leave the miner there, even though they didn't know who he was, or even how long he had been there. Miners felt a kinship with other miners, especially those who had lost their life to the dangers associated with their work. So the workers brought all of the bones out of the mine in a wheel barrow.

Daddy was appointed to be the care taker of the bones. Since my Daddy's name was Jim, it was only proper to name the skeleton after the man who took care of his bones and was in charge of the burial. That is how he became known as "Old Jim."

Daddy stored the bones in his tool shed. In his spare time he would carefully place each bone in its proper place, tying them together with a heavy thread.

Mother had asked him why he didn't bury the bones as they were, and Daddy would say, "I want all of Old Jim's bones to go in the grave with him. He should be buried in the shape of a man, like he once was."

He painstakingly tied each bone together with white thread. It took awhile for Daddy to piece him all together, it was like working a puzzle when it came to the smaller bones.

My two sisters and I were just children ourselves, and a few of our neighboring friends didn't believe there was a human skeleton in our father's tool shed, so we all took a peek inside the old shed from time to time, to see if the skeleton was complete.

It was scary enough when the bare bones of Old Jim were in a pile and only barely resembled a human frame, but when Daddy started stringing them together, it was very eerie indeed to see the boney remains of what once was a living man.

One of my older sisters, Lula would tease the younger children, especially me, telling us that the old bones were restless and would come and get us in our sleep.

As Old Jim started to look like a real human skeleton dangling from a wire in Daddy's tool shed, I began to stand at the back of the group while the other children took their turn to peek inside. I didn't want to see him as much as the other children. Even though we giggled and tried to make light of the situation, my knees trembled each time we peered inside.

On windy nights my sisters would say they could hear his bones rattling in the wind, because the cracks in the wood shed were big and one window was broken so a lot of wind could get through.

I would cover my ears to block the sound and turn my back to the window, which looked out upon the view of Daddy's tool shed off in the distance. I didn't want to look out the window, I was afraid I might see Old Jim's 'skelly' walking down to the house to get me, just like Lula had promised.

When it seemed Daddy was finally finished and had Old Jim put together, all the children got very excited, we wanted to attend the burial when Daddy laid Old Jim to rest.

One evening there were six of us children talking about how we would be happy when Old Jim was gone.

May said, "You know that skeleton really scares me!" She was the first to admit it, but each one of us nodded in agreement. She continued, "The other night I thought I saw him walking down the hillside. He stopped right by the well and looked down inside. I ran and told Paw, but when we got to the window we didn't see him anywhere."

"Your paw didn't believe you, did he?" Stanley asked. His eyes wide and round.

May confirmed he hadn't, "He made me go on to bed and said skeletons can't get up and walk." She said.

"Well, my paw said if there was a ghost, it would be trapped in the mine where they found Old Jim." Stanley told us.

My middle sister Lula spoke up, "I've heard our Daddy talking to the skeleton, I heard him say, 'Old Jim, someday I'll probably be like you, nothing but a skeleton. I'd like for someone to take care of my bones.'"

Even if the children were making the stories up, it still sent a shiver through my body. I moved a little closer to my oldest sister, Ellie, feeling only somewhat more at ease. We were standing near our house, and the tool shed wasn't too far away.

"I saw the bones get up and walk." George said and he looked the most sincere of all. "One day I snuck up to your house while no one was at home. I was going to show my cousin, 'cause he didn't believe me that your paw had a real skeleton in his tool shed. Your paw kept him hanging up, but this day Old Jim was propped up against the wall, sitting on a bench. When we looked in the window he stood straight up, you can ask my cousin! 'Cause when those old bones stood up, we took off running back to my house, and I didn't want to look in the tool shed anymore!"

Thinking back on it, George hadn't looked in the tool shed the last two times we all got together to peek inside.

I finally said to him, "I don't want to look either. I want Daddy to hurry up and bury Old Jim in the ground."

"We're going to look one last time." Lula stated, "Because Daddy said he'd be burying Old Jim in a day or two." She was already taking the first steps towards the shed.

"What if Old Jim knows he's going to be buried soon? What if he doesn't want to be buried?" May asked. Her voice was quivering, she sounded the way I felt.

Me, May and George hung back behind the others. Stanley and my two sisters were getting ahead of us.

Ellie peeked into the window first. All at once she sucked in her breath, "He's not in there!"

Lula quickly pressed up against the tool shed and looked inside, her head started shaking from side to side, "Old Jim's **not** in there!" It was said in a hurried whisper. She walked around to the door of the tool shed, ready to open the door.

"Wait a minute." May called out. She was standing close beside of me and George, "What if you let him out? Maybe he can't get out, but if you open the door you might let him out!"

"Don't open it." I begged, I was ready to make a run for the house if she did.

Lula studied the door handle, and then she looked at our sister, "You look in the window again, see if he is standing at the door."

Ellie lifted herself up on tip toes and peered inside again. "He's not in there, not that I can see."

"Let's get Daddy." I said, already leaving the group to find my father.

"Wait! You don't know where Old Jim is" George cautioned and began looking in all directions around us, searching for the skeleton.

I decided I would take my chances and took off in a run, calling for Daddy. I knew he would be around somewhere. He heard my screaming and emerged from the other side of our yard. He had a shovel in his grip. I saw him coming towards the house and I ran as fast as I could. I didn't look back to see if the others had followed me, all I wanted was to be near Daddy.

He caught me with his free hand, holding me to his side, looking confused, but it seemed my sister was running towards us fast, explaining that the bones of Old Jim were gone.

"I know." He said, with a smile curling up the corner of one side of his mouth, "I took Old Jim out to the well pump and cleaned him off a bit. He's drying out there on

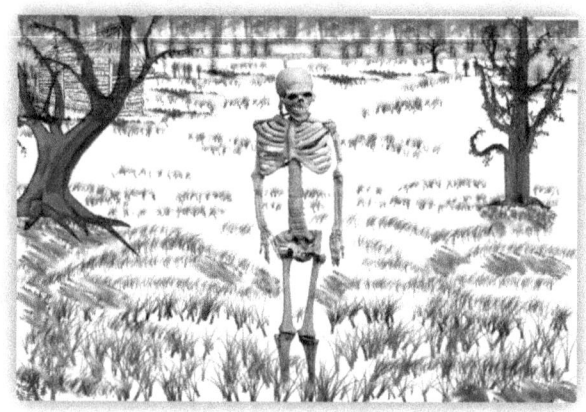

the line." And he pointed his finger in the direction of the other side of the house.

I didn't want to look, in case Old Jim wasn't there. Maybe he had gotten off the clothes line. Maybe he didn't want to be buried, like May had said.

"I've been marking the spot where I'll dig his grave. I've already made a cross, too." Daddy explained.

"Can we bury him tonight?" I pleaded.

Daddy softly chuckled, "Not tonight, but I reckon I can have his grave dug by tomorrow." Then he announced," You are each invited to the burial of Old Jim tomorrow after supper."

I went back to the house to be with Mother, I didn't want to go to the clothes line and say goodbye to Old Jim, or whatever it was the other children wanted to do. I didn't want to see him hanging on the line at all.

That night, Old Jim swayed in the wind, you could see his skeletal figure by the light of the moon. I could hear his bones rattle when the wind quickened. The noise caused me to bury my head under the covers.

He was left to dry out in the sun the next day. I didn't sleep much that night before the burial, nor did my two sisters. We took turns keeping a watchful eye on that old skeleton while the other two would try to get a little sleep.

That next day, true to his word, my Daddy got his bible and he held a burial for Old Jim. He said a prayer as a dozen people looked on; each one showing their respect for a lost miner who had been sealed in a room. Daddy said Old Jim had sat there, waiting an unknown amount of years, waiting patiently to be discovered. At least now his bones could rest in peace, along with his soul.

Daddy had made a wooden cross and carved the name "Old Jim" in the wood.

For as long as we lived there the burial spot was never disturbed, and thankfully for us children, Old Jim's bones never haunted us again.

Except on some windy nights, I could hear the hollow chime similar to what the bones had made as they bumped together from the breeze. It must have been in my memory, upon inspection there was never anything visible, and the sound would disappear in the darkness of night.

Meeting Under the Brush Arbor
By
Lavada Robbins (Copr. 2010)

Back in the mountains
When Spring came around,
We would have camp meeting
And dinner on the ground.

Shade from the Brush Arbor,
Out of the sun.
Old gospel hymns
Always were sung.

The preachers would preach about salvation.
Warn us against evil and
Giving into temptation.

Shouting and singing,
Down on our knees.
Praising our Lord,
And rejoicing in Thee.

8

<u>The Haunting of Brush Arbor</u>

As told by my mother:

Long ago in the mountains of West Virginia we would
gather for Brush Arbor, 'all day meetings and dinner on the
ground'.

Everyone from miles around would come
with their families, bringing a home cooked dish.
We spent all day under the thick shade of the
brush arbor which the men had labored to build.

It was wonderful listening to the singers; talking
with friends and listening to the preachers from other
churches preach and talk. Sometimes there would be seven
to twelve preachers there. It was a day to praise the Lord
for our spiritual growth and a day to count our blessings.

Everyone enjoyed all the old songs and the music that
would ring down the mountain side.

We all dutifully listened as the preachers told us about
salvation and explained what it would be like when we
made it to heaven.

As we lived in those mountains it seemed we were
very close to God, you could feel His presence as all the
people rejoiced in His name.

Unfortunately, there is also a dark side to life. Even though we felt we were close to heaven, there is a sadness that haunts me to this day when I think of two people who were rejected and didn't feel the joy that we all experienced at Brush Arbor.

The memory of the two lone figures has always remained in the minds of many, especially in my mind.

I was a small child myself at the time this story unfolds. I can still envision Eve. That was not her real name, but much like Eve of the Bible who was blamed for sin, so was this Eve.

You see, she was only between the age of eleven and twelve when she gave birth to a baby boy out of wedlock.

I can still envision her standing away from the crowd with her long brown hair flowing down over her shoulders. She often wore a long dress down to her shoes. She mostly held tight to her little boy's hand, watching from afar.

Eve was not welcome in the crowd and wasn't allowed to speak to any of the young children. Even our mother would tell us not to play with her, or to have anything to do with her because she was a "bad girl".

As a young child myself I didn't know the exact definition of 'good' or 'bad' people, I only knew what I saw and heard others say about Eve.

Later, as I recalled how she and her son were treated, abandoned by the whole camp, including the preachers, I wondered what the innocent boy child had ever done to deserve being an out-cast. In my later years I wondered what Eve had done to deserve being judged and treated so harshly. From the beginning of time, until time will end, there will be those who make similar mistakes.

I often tried to imagine how Eve must have felt, forsaken by everyone including her parents. Although they had given her a home, there was never an outward sign of love or support.

Especially on the day of Brush Arbor, with all of the singing and preaching, I pondered how she had felt about herself, and how she felt about the people of the mountains; especially on that day, when we were all suppose to be rejoicing in the Lord, and counting our blessings.

Hardly anyone ever spoke to her. That explains how no one would have realized when the thoughts of suicide or murder began to ravage her mind. Had she been thinking about it for a long while? Or had the thought come to her on that day at Brush Arbor? The last day anyone could recall seeing her alive.

Many days later, when some men were hunting, they smelled a horrible stench. They could tell that it came from below the bluff. One man thought he saw crumpled clothing discarded on the ground at the foot of the bluff. When they descended the side of the mountain to investigate, there were the remains of Eve and her son.

It was clear they had been dead for several days, as flies and maggots worked on the bodies, and the odor became overwhelming, forcing the men to cover their faces. The men hurried to the campsite and sent for help.

It was Ben who delivered the bad news to Eve's parents. Later he would say they didn't seem too upset. Her father had said, "I guess she couldn't face the shame and guilt of having a baby out of wedlock."

One of the preachers, Mr. Smith, said it was difficult for him to preach at the funeral of two so young, but he warned us all to "Let this be a lesson, a life waged in sin will bring much shame and disgrace upon a family and upon an entire camp. The wages of sin is always death. The heavy weight of her sin drove Eve to kill her innocent son and take her own life, which wasn't hers to take."

I remember looking around at the people who attended the funeral, watching as some wept and others just stood in silence. I wondered if they felt the same as me.

I kept wondering where the father of Eve's son was. Who was he, and was he among the crowd?

I watched as the small casket was placed into the ground, trying to match a face with similar features to the boy who was now being buried at such a young age. It wouldn't be the last time I was curious about whom the father was, and curious about why he hadn't been rejected and ridiculed the same as Eve.

As time passed there were whispers from the people of the mountains, asking why the family had never reported Eve and her son missing before their bodies were found. This raised much suspicion.

There were also very hushed whispers speculating about the identity of the father of the young boy. But this was something discussed only between adults, as the children were never allowed to speak of such things.

One day during recess at school I heard that Eve's mother had become very ill. Even at my age I couldn't accept that it was from heart break, since the woman never showed any outward love towards Eve or her son.

It was a girl named Mattie who told what she had seen, "That poor old woman's hair has turned almost white!" She said, "Every night she goes out to where the bodies were found, just looking over the edge, pacing back and forth."

Some of the older children heard Mattie talking, so they decided to go out to the bluff and see if Eve's mother was white haired.

I had two older sisters, Lula and Ellie, who was about the age of Eve, and I asked Ellie if she knew anything about it.

"You can't talk about it." Ellie warned, "Or she'll come after you."

"Who?" I asked, because I didn't think Eve's mother would come after anyone.

"Eve! Her spirit is walking around! It is visiting the people who were mean to her. Especially her parents."

At my age, I was too terrified to ask anymore about it, I didn't want a ghost coming after me.

A few days later Mattie was telling the small children what she had learned, "That old woman is trying to find her daughter's ghost!" She told us, and we all seemed to shiver from a cold draft at the same time.

Someone spoke up and asked Mattie how she knew, and she explained that her brother was one of the children who spied on Eve's parents. They had followed the mother out to the bluff and watched as she paced back and forth, crying and talking to Eve, calling her name, asking her to please go on and leave them alone.

It didn't take long before almost everyone in the camp knew that Eve was haunting her family, and there had been some mention that even one of the preachers had been visited by her specter.

They said that Eve's mother was looking more aged day by day, and her father wasn't doing well, either. His pants were sagging a little more and he seemed to be a little stooped. The men who worked with him said he had become quiet; he wouldn't talk much to anyone.

Finally it was getting closer to Brush Arbor day again. The construction of the brush structure was complete.

This year as the mourner's bench was carried out to the campsite many people speculated who would use it. Of course the names of Eve's parents came up more than once.

Ed and Francine were their names, and even though much of the attention had shifted focus from them to other matters that had arisen during the year, a lot of people were confident those two people would be the first to the bench.

It was true that Francine's hair was almost white, and it seemed she had aged twenty years since the last big meeting. She was standing next to her husband, and he looked as if he had lost a lot of weight, just like everyone had said. He slumped as though a heavy weight was on his shoulders.

My mother told me to stop staring, but she was watching almost as much as I was.

Ed and Francine didn't attend church much, so it wasn't too often that I ever saw them, but on this day, most eyes were upon them. I sensed it was making them both nervous.

The meeting began like any other camp meeting and the children were off to enjoy the festivities. As the evening wore on and the first preacher was about to speak, a huge crowd had gathered.

The preacher began talking and his voice was getting louder as he spoke of the promise land. As the preacher's sermon got underway there were mourners that came to the bench, there was shouting and rejoicing and screams of praise, so it easily went unnoticed for awhile that a woman had fainted.

It was common for women to faint at these functions, but when Aggie Sanders started pointing and screaming; her feet almost stomping a hole in the ground, she caught the attention of the preacher.

When the preacher paused and strained to see what was going on, we all turned to look.

You could see the crowd parting, moving away from something among them. They wore faces of shock as silence fell over the people.

I didn't get to see it, but I heard everyone later talking about it, how a misty, dingy white form glided right up to Ed and he started backing away, muttering and spitting all over himself. Francine fainted alongside another woman, and Aggie Sanders nearly fell into the arms of the person next to her, with face pale and gray.

The preacher began to sweat, and his face was getting red as he started praying.

My mother put her arm over my shoulder and around the shoulder of one of my sisters and told us to bow our heads and pray.

The preacher was saying there was "evil among us" and that someone had to repent. I can't recall a more heated sermon, as the preacher shouted and prayed and begged for all of our forgiveness.

A few men took Ed and Francine inside, out of the crowd, along with Aggie and the fainted woman.

The next day word quickly spread that Ed had repeatedly warned, "She's come back to take our souls to hell!"

Two of the visiting preachers met with Ed and Francine and prayed for their healing. But it was said that the prayers didn't seem to bring peace to the fearful parents.

Some of the women folk stayed with Ed and Francine for a few days afterwards, and each of the women reported the same thing. It was no wonder the couple was in the condition they were in. There was simply no peace in their house. The fire wouldn't stay lit for very long in the fireplace, a sudden, cold draft would extinguish it every night. The same was true of candles and oil lamps. If Ed would light one, before long a mysterious draft would blow out the flame.

Not only that, but there were no pictures or mirrors on any of the walls. Francine had told the women that the pictures would fall from the walls and break in the floor, startling them in the process, as it usually happened late at night when she and Ed were sleeping.

One of the women took it upon herself to tell Preacher Smith of the strange occurrences. Mr. Smith believed it was the restless spirit of their daughter Eve, especially after the mysterious mist had approached Ed right in front of people on Brush Arbor day.

Mr. Smith and a deacon of the church decided it was time to visit the parents, in hopes of helping them. He later told that Ed was not pleased by the visit, he didn't appreciate their interference, but that Francine seemed to want their help.

Mr. Smith and the deacon prayed with Ed and Francine that night and cleansed their home with holy water. But when he left, Mr. Smith said he saw an off-white mist, hovering a few feet off the ground just on the other side of the house. He said it sent shivers up his spine. He had tried to show the deacon, but the misty apparition evaporated before the other man could see it.

After that night, few people saw Ed or Francine.

Even though Ed reported to work as usual, he didn't want to talk to anyone, and he would leave as soon as his labor was done, hurrying home. Francine wouldn't speak much either, and was rarely seen in public.

The behavior of Eve's parents and the fact that many people in the mountains had seen the misty apparition near her house gave way to horrid speculation.

A few people reported seeing a misty specter at the bluff where Eve and her son's body had been found. But since the apparition was most often witnessed at the home of Eve's parents, most of the people had come to believe that this was the spot where Eve and her son had actually died.

This fueled rumors that Ed had killed them and flung their bodies over the side of the mountain to make it look like a suicide/murder, brought on by the shame of Eve having a baby out of wedlock. A lot of people thought Eve hadn't named the father of the boy because she didn't know who he was. Of course such rumors could embarrass a family.

Yet there were those who thought maybe Eve hadn't named the father because he was a married man, and maybe **he** had killed her and the innocent boy, dumping their bodies over the bluff so no one could ever discover his identity.

The next year at the Brush Arbor meeting, Ed nor Francine attended. The preachers took their turns preaching, and it seemed it was going to be a normal evening; Until Preacher Smith took his turn at the stand.

He seemed a little nervous as he approached the bench. He began with a thankful prayer for blessings, asking God to help the families in the camp, for all those with special needs that only God knew about.

Then he started talking about forgiveness, and as he quoted scriptures from the bible, he started to stammer and stutter, his eyes growing wide as the color drained from his face.

People looked to each other for the answers for his behavior. The answer was just behind them.

Many people said they saw the hovering misty shape as it approached. They say it took the form of what appeared to be mother and child, approaching the crowd from the distance. Others didn't see anything; they only heard a commotion and tried to locate the disturbance.

The only thing I can remember is that there was a very cold draft which moved through the crowd that night, and preacher Smith kneeled down, tears streaming down his face, praying to God to forgive every person in the camp for what they had done wrong, for they had brought this upon themselves, and he prayed that the spirits who were haunting Brush Arbor would return to the Lord and be at peace.

Women cried and men kept their heads bowed, most of the children looked to their parents, trying to understand what was taking place.

Only after that day did it become clear that Mr. Smith knew why the spirit kept returning.

Within a few days of that Brush Arbor meeting Ed and Francine packed up and moved out of the mountains, and though the rumors continued to circulate that it was them Eve was haunting, every once in awhile the misty apparition would still make itself known to one of the townspeople. The tale would travel fast through the mountains and before the next day everyone seemed to know that Eve had not met her peace. Many say she wouldn't find rest until every last person who had wronged her would face their guilt from fear of her haunt, and would seek forgiveness for how they had judged her and turned away from her and the innocent child.

9

Grandma Spirit

Mountain folk are intelligent, sensible people. They believe in God and they know He is real. They don't question His ways, or question how He may warn them of events to come. The people of the mountain recognize that He has angels everywhere. Many don't consider this superstition, they consider it faith. Yet there are those who would say this story is about mountain superstition.

From my Mother:

I was raised in the mountains of West Virginia in a coal camp community. Winters were cold and snowy. In order to stay warm we would live in two rooms of our house, with only two beds for the five of us. Our only source of heat was a fireplace with a grate and mantle.

Mother would hang bed sheets and quilts over doorways to the other rooms, draping quilts over the windows to keep out the cold air. The kitchen and bedroom were the only two rooms we heated in the winter months.

I was the youngest of three girls, as this was before our little brother was born. I always slept between my two older sisters. Since I was small they were afraid if the fire went out during the night that I could freeze to death. In the mountains the temperature could dip down to five degrees below zero.

Daddy and Mother slept in the other bed. We had a heavy quilt on both of our beds. It seemed so heavy to me that it was hard to turn over. I had to work hard to get out of bed with that much cover on us, especially being sandwiched between Lula and Ellie.

One night I was breathless, I awakened to a choking feeling. I woke up trying to catch my breath. It may have been the heavy covers on the bed, or because one of my sisters had thrown an arm over my face, but I felt smothered. No matter what had aroused me, I propped myself up on my left elbow, with my hand under my head, catching my breath.

I spent several minutes looking at the fireplace, immediately calming down and was able to breathe a little easier. I watched the dancing flames, and noticed how Daddy always banked the fire in hopes of having heat in our house all night. The fire emitted a cast of soft light in the room, providing a warm yellowish glow.

I watched the flames, which were crackling and flickering in constant motion. Then a shadow moved and caught my attention. To the right of the mantle stood the shadowy figure of a person, stooped forward as though she was looking in the fireplace. It was a womanly figure; I could see the outline of her hair, illuminated by the light from the fire. I thought it must be my mother stoking the fire.

But then my mother spoke to me from her bed and asked what was wrong, was I sick or did I need to get up and use the slop jar?

I said, "No. I'm watching that woman standing at the fireplace."

I was probably only seven years old, and for some reason I was not startled by this vision.

My mother said rather calmly, "You must be having a bad dream, go back to sleep, Asharah, there is no one there."

I looked at the fireplace, at the woman who was now facing in our direction. Though her features were not clear she was still visible, "No, Mother, I still see her, there is a woman standing there."

Mother raised up in bed, she was also looking at the fireplace, in the direction of the woman. She asked, "Describe her to me?"

I could see this lady, more of a silhouette than a clear image, yet I could make out certain features as the flames danced and cast a soft glow across her face, "She has hair longer than yours. She is tall and slim. She has high cheek bones." I explained as I watched the womanly figure.

My mother was silent for only a moment, "You are dreaming, Asharah. I do not see anyone there. Please go back to sleep." My mother turned away from the fireplace and lay back down.

I looked back at the fireplace and the woman was gone. I decided that my mother was right, maybe I had been dreaming.

The next morning Mother was acting peculiar and appeared worried about something. She was making our breakfast and seemed nervous as I caught her looking over her shoulder at the slightest noise, looking for something, or someone.

In the mountains when someone sees a ghost or an unusual vision, many believe it to be a warning. The old 'wives tale' is that someone in the family would die after such a vision. Since Daddy worked in the coal mines, Mother spent her life knowing that when he left in the morning it could very well be the last time she would see him alive. There had been blasts that sealed mine shafts, trapping men inside. Some men even died from the force of the explosion. There had also been slate cave-ins, crushing miners while they worked. There were so many things that could go wrong, and had gone wrong in the past.

Mother believed that since her youngest daughter had an unexpected vision of a woman that it must be a warning of some kind. She had always been told that young children could see angels to the age of credibility. Mother believed she was being forewarned, and she was worried all that day.

She didn't want to frighten her children, so she didn't mention her concerns that morning. It was after Daddy came home safely that evening and she could breathe a sigh of relief that she felt more at ease to talk about it.

The family was at home together, and Mother seemed calmer than she had earlier. She told Daddy of my 'dream', as she called it, and he listened intently. He was calm as he explained, "If it was a dream, maybe it was a visit from a departed loved one. Either way, we are blessed here tonight, and we should remember to be thankful."

The next evening Mother said she would like to ask me about what I thought I saw the other night at the fireplace. She asked me again to describe the woman to her.

As I described the woman, my Mother carefully explained, "When I was about your age my mother passed away. You have never seen her, or even a picture of her, but you are describing my mother and how she looked before she died." Her eyes seemed to sadden as she talked about her. "You see, I believe it was my mother who visited that night, but she woke up the wrong little girl. Sometimes God sends angels as familiar spirits to help those of us with a heavy heart." My mother reached out and patted my hand, her eyes glistening as she smiled, "I've always missed my mother. It is nice to know she may be watching over us." Mother spoke gently, "I am thankful you saw her spirit. I was afraid something horrible was going to happen, but instead, she let me know everything is going to be alright."

From her dress pocket she withdrew a tattered photograph, handing it to me. "Could this be the woman you saw?"

I looked at the faded picture of a woman who appeared to be tall and slender, with very dark hair, just like the woman at the fireplace. Though I couldn't make out the features, it seemed she had large, dark eyes and very high cheekbones. "This is her." I stated firmly, because I believed it to be so.

Mother took back the picture, "She is watching over us." She said and her words warmed me from the inside.

After seeing the photograph of my grandmother, I have felt confident that God has a way of sending angels to help us through our times of need.

It was during a time in my mother's life that she lived with the fear of losing her husband. This fear had become a heavy burden to carry. After that nightly visit, Mother and our family seemed more comfortable that Daddy was going to be safe in the mines.

I know I wasn't dreaming on that fateful night long ago. I believe I saw my Grandma's spirit. That would explain why even when I should have felt alarm, I felt at ease looking at the kind woman standing at the fireplace.

———————————————

Superstition, Faith or Luck?

Superstitions have been around for centuries. Superstitions can be defined as old wives tales, folklore, bizarre beliefs, taboos, omens, lucky & unlucky things.

An example would be wearing or carrying a charm; carrying a rabbit's foot; hanging a horse shoe above your door for good luck or to avoid bad luck.

Most of us know that we should go in another direction when a black cat crosses our path. We are cautioned never walk under a ladder, or sweep your house after the sun goes down. If we spill salt we might be tempted to toss some over our shoulder to avoid bad luck, just in case.

These are old wives tales that have been handed down through the generations. Even if we don't believe in them, most of us know about some of them.

My mother shared a true story with me that might fall under the definition of a superstition or maybe it falls under the definition of "faith." I will let you be the judge.

10

Dead Man's Bones

As told by my mother:

Superstitions are still around today, and it is not only the poor or uneducated people who believe you can wear or carry something to bring good luck.

Well educated, decent people, even Hollywood stars seek out fortune tellers or psychics. They pay money to have their fortunes read in search of what the future holds in store for them. They read books about psychic energy and influences.

The Bible even mentions in Exodus 32, where the children of Israel asked Aaron to make a golden calf as a symbolism of a god for them to worship. They needed a sign. Some people are like that even today.

When we face misfortune or delays, anxieties or worry, when we don't know where the next meal is coming from, sometimes we find ourselves grasping at any straw we think might bring us good luck. This is possibly one of the reasons my father took such a chance back during the Great Depression.

In the late 1920's and early 1930's, everyone was in desperate need. Men and women stood in line all day to get rations of food for their families. These were the times when my Daddy would leave the house in the early morning, toting a sack he would carry every day, so that if he found something to eat, such as an abandoned garden where someone had moved away, he could pull up turnips, onions, or potatoes from the ground. In the sack would go walnuts, hazelnuts or hickory nuts, which he would bring home to his family.

Daddy was a God fearing man who believed in the power of prayer. When he prayed, he went down on his knees and he talked to God daily.

In the early spring during the depression, Daddy didn't have a job; he worked what he could on the W.P.A.. In 1935, the government gave him a job on the C.C.C. which was a government project. But these were temporary jobs, and were scheduled to end soon.

One day as he was plowing his garden, a man Daddy knew approached him and talked for a bit then he asked, "Are you down on your luck? I have just the thing you need that will bring you good luck." He was carrying a small box which he didn't open at that moment.

Daddy informed him he didn't believe in charms or luck or anything like that.

"But Jim, let me tell you about what I have, then you can make up your mind. I believe it would be of great benefit to you and your family and after you hear about it you might want to buy it."

Daddy thought to himself that he only had fifty cents to his name, he had a family depending on him, but he also recognized that this man was trying to make money for his own family and children to feed. He also knew that God was good, and if the man needed the money so desperately and if he could help another, God would provide for both his family and the man's family.

He would listen to the man and at least give him a chance, so he invited him to sit on the porch and explain what he had to offer.

"Jim, if you take what is in this little box, and follow the instructions, carry it with you always, you will have good luck and always have what your family needs. But you can never look inside the pouch; it must never be opened by you or anyone." The man paused and looked deep into Jim's eyes, "I don't even know what is in it, but I know that it is sold at Indian reservations and many Indians believe and carry such a bag. I have started to carry one, myself. I trust that my luck will improve and my family will have all that we need."

Jim studied the man for a minute, "I only have fifty cents." He spoke, "That's all I have."

"Then I will take that much for it." He handed Jim the box, "May you have good luck and good health all the days of your life."

Daddy took the little box inside to Mother, and told her about the man and admitted that he had spent his last fifty cents for it.

"Jim, there must be something wrong with you to spend your last penny on something like that!" She scolded.

"But sweetheart, he has little children like me to feed, and right now we have food to eat. We have just enough for our family. God wants us to share and help others. I believe in God, and God sent that man to our house for a reason. Maybe so we could help him."

Though Mother wasn't too pleased with the transaction, she opened the box which contained a little, thin pouch that had small unknown objects inside of it. The odd shaped contents felt similar to little sticks, twigs and pebbles.

She didn't open it, she followed the instructions which said to use red flannel, cutting two squares about 3 inches by 2 inches and to sew a little bag to put the thin pouch

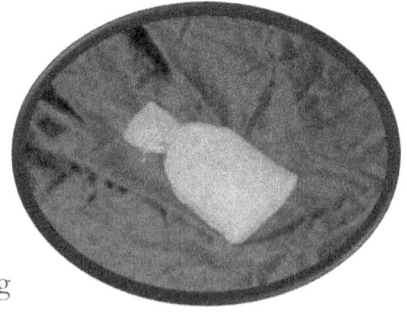

inside, and then she tied it tightly, stitching the pouch closed never to be opened again. The instructions said to wear it in a pocket, or carry it every day.

We now know that an amulet is something to be worn or carried to guard against evil, to protect from harm or disease. Back in those days we didn't know anything about an amulet so we children called the pouch and its contents Daddy's "Dead Man's Bones." To our small fingers, the contents felt like small, hard bones.

We respected our father and the pouch; we were told never to open it or play with it.

Daddy carried it with him every day, and at night when he retired to bed he would leave it safely on his dresser.

When my two older sisters grew old enough to work and needed to look for a job, they took Daddy's Dead Man's Bones, thinking the pouch of bones could help them get a job when they went to the unemployment office.

The bones didn't go inside the unemployment office that day. The girls went inside and applied for their job, neither of them feeling very lucky. They both wondered why the good luck charm hadn't worked for them, as it had worked for their father. It was when they came out of the unemployment office that the older one, Ellie questioned, "Isn't that Daddy's Dead Man's Bones there on the steps?"

"Yes it is. How did it get there?" The younger one, Lula, picked the pouch up and placed it safely in her pocket, feeling guilty that they had taken the bones to use for their gain.

"We won't ever take them again." They promised one another. After they got home, the girls admitted what they had done, and they made the same promise to Daddy.

Our father was saddened that his daughters took the pouch without permission, but he accepted their apology and explained that faith was what brought him his good fortune, not luck.

You see, when Daddy bought the pouch, he didn't have a job and the mining company wouldn't hire him because of an old coal mining injury on his leg, which could get mine poisoning in the open wound, so the mining company couldn't take a chance like that.

After he bought the bones, things did get better and we eventually moved out of the mountains. Though our family was never wealthy, we always had everything we needed, and Daddy never went without employment again.

Both Mother and Daddy lived long lives. The bones stayed with Daddy until his death and then they passed to Mother until her death. When she died they passed to me, the youngest girl; I became the keeper of the red, flannel bag called "Dead Man's Bones."

Daddy was not superstitious and neither am I, but the "Dead Man's Bones" are an icon that mean a lot to me, as they remind me of my dear father. They also remind me that by giving as Daddy had, even in a time when his family needed, and by trusting in God and His power, that the goodness will be returned. The power of that belief cannot be questioned even to this day. For Daddy spent his last penny on them and never needed a job again.

One time when I worked in a shop not too many years ago, there was a lady psychic giving readings for a one day event. I was not there for a reading, as I worked behind the counter, and furthermore didn't exactly believe in psychics.

She approached me and said, "I would not attempt to give you a psychic reading."

I asked her why.

She answered, "You have something on you that produces an aura, one that I would not try to read."

I thought for a moment and I knew it must be the Dead Man's Bones. "I have something that has been in my family for years." I told her and pulled out the little red pouch. "It has never been opened. I don't know what is inside."

I placed it in her palm and she cupped it gently between her two hands, holding it away from her. Looking at me she said, "I feel a warm energy. It is a good energy. I don't know where the energy comes from, or what could be inside the bag, but it is very unique."

I took the pouch that was stained on one side from where my Daddy had worn it inside his shirt pocket and the coal dust had stained it over the years. There was a warm feeling that I got when I held it, too, but I

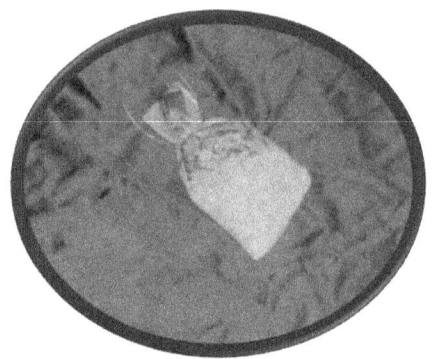

This is the actual pouch known as "Dead Man's Bones". It has been in our family for generations. The coal stains are still on one side where it was worn in Jim's shirt pocket all those years.

always thought that feeling must have come from love.

An **amulet**, meaning "an object that protects a person from trouble." Consists of any object intended to bring good <u>luck</u> and/or protection to its owner. Can be worn on the body, hanging from the neck or strapped to the arm or leg, they may also serve as protective emblems on walls and doorways.

Ghost stories and superstitions are not just confined to the mountains or rural areas. In the minds of many, including the author of this book, the possibility of spiritual visitors from the other side can happen anywhere, or to anyone. In many events it can be a feeling or sensation that someone is around even when we're all alone. Until the moment something unexplainable happens, or we see something to validate our feelings, a haunting can be dismissed as an over active imagination. This story takes place in Anderson County, TN in our modern times.

11

<u>The Estate Sale</u>

As told by my mother:

Estate sales have always fascinated me. I especially love old jewelry, old furniture, old books, the older the better. Aged second hand jewelry with real stones have a lot of beauty and charm; each has a story of its own. From the craftsman's specialty, who puts every little stone in place with loving care, to the time when it is finally placed around a woman's neck or on her finger when she promises marriage to the man she loves, a story can unfold about each piece of jewelry.

A necklace given as an anniversary gift after years of marriage is such an occasion where there is a lot of emotional energy that could possibly transfer from people to objects.

Each necklace or ring, even if made from shell gold has its own special shine and allure. It is the giving and receiving that makes each piece of jewelry so special when it is given with love.

At estate sales I am always drawn to the old jewelry first. At this particular estate sale a certain necklace fascinated me with its little amber stones and hair-net mesh work that delicately held each tiny stone in place.

Some of the mesh had come apart, but all the stones appeared to be accounted for. They glittered and glowed and sparkled as if to be greeting me, silently asking me to buy this charming necklace.

Purchasing the necklace aroused an excitement within me and I couldn't wait to get home and look at it through my magnifying glass. I could simply sit for hours looking at this beautiful old necklace and the sparkles it created, fingering the delicate mesh, touching the small amber jewels, admiring the craftsmanship and detail of the necklace. Maybe the fascination ignited my imagination, feeling as though someone or something was looking over my shoulder and approving of my care and love for the necklace.

I knew it was silly even thinking that there was some hidden mystery or a supernatural force at work, but when I wore the necklace, or gave any attention to it, I felt a change in my demeanor, and I also felt a presence, a good presence. But as time passed and I turned my attention to other things the atmosphere changed within my home. Then little things begin to get moved from where I had placed them.

For instance, a photo album of my children and family that I carried in my pocket-book went missing, and my mother's scrap book did, too. I wanted to read my granddaughter a poem from the book and when I went to the location where I always kept it, the scrap book was no longer there. I searched for two days and finally found it in my mother's old record box where I would never put it.

As for the photo album that I kept in my purse, it took a week to find it and then it was right under my nose, in plain view in a small bedroom I use as an office. I know I had looked there more than once for it.

That was just the beginning of things to be moved. For instance my ankle boots, I looked for them for two years before I finally found them in a location where I never would have put them. Coincidentally, these boots were bought at an estate sale, as many of my favorite items are found at private sales. It seemed that somebody or something didn't like for me to spend time on anything except looking at, wearing or adoring the necklace. For when I did look at it, or wear it, there seemed to be peaceful, pleasant atmosphere surround me.

It didn't make sense to me, but in order to find some answers I knew I had to go back to the beginning, which was the estate sale. I needed to acquire some history on this necklace that seemed to charm me. I wanted to know about the woman who had owned the necklace prior.

It had been four years since I bought the necklace at the estate sale, so my chance of finding someone who knew the history was as slim as finding a needle in a haystack.

I had looked very closely that night at the necklace, hoping to get a sense of where to start. It seemed I didn't need to look far for the answers, the answers found me.

Sunday morning arrived and I always match the colors in my outfit with jewels, pins, earrings and necklace. This Sunday I selected a dress with a small amount of amber in the pattern. To bring the color out I needed amber jewels, which wasn't a problem, as the necklace I kept pinned on a cushion was perfect.

I hadn't mended the mesh tear that was in it, the necklace was exactly in the same condition as when I bought it. Would anyone see it or would this small flaw be concealed in the stones? When I had worn the necklace in the past I always got compliments on it, so it seemed few people, if any, ever noticed the small imperfection.

In church that Sunday a lady sitting behind me tapped my shoulder and asked about the necklace I was wearing. She said it looked like the one her aunt had years ago, and she had never seen another like it. I was very excited when she mentioned her aunt's necklace, so I asked her if we could talk after church and she agreed.

After church we met in the parking lot. I took the necklace off and she looked it over. She said it must be her aunt's necklace, because hers had also been torn in the mesh work. She said her aunt had worn the necklace day and night after her husband died, as it was the last anniversary present he had given her.

I asked about her aunt and uncle, what they were like.

She said her aunt was a petite woman who was always happy. She loved her family and husband very much. She described, "My uncle was a tall, slender man and very good looking. He was a kind man who loved his wife. He took very good care of his wife and family. He died about a year before my aunt died. My family thought his sudden passing might have hastened her death, we believe she grieved herself to death.

"That necklace was given to her for their wedding anniversary the year he died. She always wore it, and I think it should have been buried with her. But it was overlooked and was sold at an estate sale." She explained.

I thanked her for taking the time and sharing the information. I brought the necklace back home, pinning it back on the cushion with a new appreciation for the jewelry and the sentiment attached to it.

Each night when I would turn the lights on every little stone would twinkle like stars in the night sky. It seemed to emit a warm feeling of adoration and I would think of the charming couple, so much in love. I would imagine how happy they must have been on their anniversary when the husband had lovingly placed the necklace around his wife's neck.

One night soon after, I woke up from a deep sleep. I felt the presence of someone in my bedroom, and there at the foot of my bed was this tall, slim shadow of a man.

Chills ran up and down my body as thoughts raced through my mind. Had I left the door unlocked and an intruder had come inside? I wanted to sink deep under the bed covers and become invisible, but the shadowy figure was walking away.

With my heart beating loudly in my chest, I knew I had to get up and find out who was in my house.

I always kept a ball bat under my bed and I quietly reached for it, gripping it in my hands. The nearest phone was in my kitchen, another in my living room. I eased out of bed to make my way to a telephone.

I felt less threatened as I went from room to room, turning on lights as I looked. Revealing that there was no one in the house, and the doors and windows were all locked tight.

Returning to my bedroom a sparkle caught my eye. I looked at the necklace. Somehow I knew who my intruder had been. He had been visiting all along; watching carefully over his wife's most treasured possession.

I gently touched the necklace, and spoke aloud, "I will love this necklace and take good care of it." I promised.

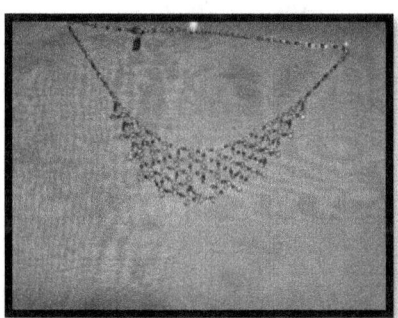

Actual photo of the necklace this story is based on.

From that night on, nothing else went missing or was misplaced in my house. The necklace is still pinned on the cushion on my dresser when I am not wearing it, and someday soon I will mend it. But for now it is a splendid way to remember a couple so much in love that in even death their love survives.

Hauntings

Tragedy or premature death is often a precursor to a haunting, as are murder and suicide. Would all 4 components guarantee a haunting? Or would it simply make an interesting story for generations to tell over a campfire, or share with friends at Halloween?

Some say either you are a believer or you are a skeptic. But I believe you can be a little bit of both. After all, there are reasonable explanations for much of the mystery that surrounds the Stansbury house. Yet there is a larger element of the story that simply can't be explained.

Even if you are one who does not believe, this tale may convince you to think twice about hauntings.

The house known by another name still stands majestically atop a privately owned knoll in Tennessee.

It has changed ownership many times over the years with extended periods of vacancies when the yard and shrubs would become over gown and the intricate details of the wood trim would become weather damaged and rotted in some spots.

At one time it was boarded up and the community wanted to see it condemned. Each time a new owner bought and restored the beautiful structure, the house seemed to become even more picturesque.

The only downside is the strange phenomenon which occurs regularly. Maybe those strange events can be explained with this story.

Names have been changed to protect any remaining family members.

12

The Stansbury Legacy

Tucked away in a very rural area of East Tennessee, stands an old mansion. In the late eighteenth century this home was built by a doctor who relocated to Tennessee just before the turn of the nineteenth century.

His name was Dr. Stansbury, and he had the home built to meet his needs. Those needs proved to be many.

The house had six bedrooms, at that time was considered a mansion as it was more than three thousand square feet on the main level living. It also had a basement, which was constructed as his office/clinic. The attic area was finished as living quarters for his servant.

It is claimed there was no wasted space anywhere, and in fact, there were more rooms than the floor plan called for. Secret rooms, small alcoves that only the doctor had use for.

Dr. Stansbury had selected this town in the Southeast to help the less fortunate, at that time there wasn't an area physician.

Most agree that he was a kind man, but he had a mental problem. Though it was never documented, judging from this story it is plausible to say the least.

His name was Clyde and his wife was Faye, and together they raised four children. It seemed Faye was a delicate woman and had difficulty carrying babies to term.

Her first two pregnancies had resulted in miscarriage in the second trimesters. In both cases the babies were delivered around five months of pregnancy and neither child had survived.

It wasn't until both Faye and Clyde passed away that the townspeople discovered the two fetuses preserved in a medical container, or jar, stored safely in a hidden alcove of Dr. Stansbury's basement. The names on the containers identified the babies as "Elizabeth Amelia" and the other baby was "Charles Edward."

The Stansbury's eventually raised four more children, but the children were spaced many years apart. Kyle Edmond was the oldest and his brother immediately following him was four years younger. The daughter that followed was again almost four years separated, while the youngest daughter came along six years later.

It is said that though each family member was polite and mannerly the entire family seemed distant to one another, there didn't seem to be a bond that connected any of them.

The mansion was a sight to behold atop a grassy knoll, at the foothills of one mountain, perched atop a small peak looking down upon the town, yet obscured and protected in its own right by distance and acreage.

The lights could be seen burning in the windows at night, but it was a decent walk or ride from even the nearest neighbor to pay the old Doctor a visit. From the house to the road was approximately one mile and the acreage that surrounded the home belonged to Dr. Stansbury.

The town was delighted when the doctor built his home here, as the nearest physician had been in the neighboring city. The Stansburys invited the entire town to come out when the home was complete, to meet the doctor and his family and his humble servant Beaula.

There wasn't a house in the town at the time that could compare to the magnificence of this stone fortress, thereby most of the town's people turned out to see the house, while at the same time meeting their new doctor.

It didn't take long for Dr. Stansbury's medical practice to prosper. He regularly employed at least 2 nurses, while his wife answered the phones.

Though Beaula took care of the living quarters, in the manner of cleaning, cooking and serving meals, he had hired another for keeping his office clean. The only servant to reside there was Beaula.

Dr. Stansbury not only treated his patients for the common cold, he delivered babies, treated knife wounds and gunshot wounds and performed minor surgeries in his home office.

Many thought he was a bit too experimental, but the community supported their doctor. After all, he was a very intelligent man and he came from a family of physicians. He bragged that he had helped his father tend to wounded soldiers when he was only nine years old. He didn't know any other way of life, in fact.

So he was quickly forgiven when he lost patients during surgeries, or when he tried experimental treatments that often resulted in death or paralysis, or the inability to speak; and there were many such patients this happened to.

Still yet, he was appreciated by most because he was kind enough to donate his guest room to those who required short term stay.

He also donated a large parcel of his land to be designated as a cemetery for the families who were simply too poor to afford a proper burial. It wasn't until after his death that the town's folks started to speak negatively about these things, always adding that though he was generous, it was mostly **his** patients that filled the cemetery.

Beaula was quiet and respectful of her employer and his family, she seemed to genuinely like most of the Stansburys. It wasn't until she fell in love with a local grocer that she even started to speak about the inner workings of the Stansbury life. At first it was little tidbits of information that she shared with Archie after he asked her out and she turned him down.

"Oh, the Mister and Missus won't let me off to go out with you." She told him.

"You work all seven days?" Archie asked.

"Mostly." Beaula affirmed, "I'm supposed to be off on Sundays, but when a baby is to be born, or someone is facing life or death, sometimes I still have to work, 'cause Missus has to help her husband sometimes and I have to look after the children."

"You should have time for yourself." Archie scoffed. He didn't give up, though, almost every week when Beaula came to buy groceries he asked her out on a date. He liked Beaula, she was a kind soul, with large, warm eyes.

It took awhile, but she finally agreed and on Sundays they made it a regular date to meet after church and go up to the lookout and have a picnic. Except when there was an emergency at Dr. Stansbury's.

Archie and Beaula had a long courtship. It could have been because Beaula was faithful to her position in the

Stansbury family, or it could have been that since they only saw each other privately one day each week and not always then, that it took a long time to get to know one another well enough for Archie to propose.

It was nearly a three year long courtship. But Archie did finally propose and he had it all planned out, too. Because how could a marriage work if he only saw his wife four times a month?

"You can have a job in the grocery store with me, we can always use some help, especially around the holidays."

Beaula was clearly excited because she loved Archie, he made her feel safe and happy all at the same time. But how could she ever leave the Stansburys? "Archie, I've been with Mister and the Missus since I was sixteen years old. They rescued me from an orphanage." Then she dropped her chin and looked at her hands, which she had the habit of rubbing them together when she got nervous, "Besides, you want a family of your own, don't ya?"

Archie said he did, "We aren't getting any younger Beaula. But you're still young enough to give me a child." He reminded, "I know we're starting late, but I love you, Beaula."

"That's not it." Beaula told him, struggling to find the words, "I can't give you a child." She admitted with guilt.

Archie wasn't sure how to respond, but he knew he

loved her, "That's alright, if you can't… I mean, do we really know until we've tried?" Archie knew she had never been married before, although she had been courted a time or two, most of her life had been very sheltered.

Beaula had looked at him for a long moment and it seemed there were tears welling in her eyes, but Archie later told that she pulled her chin up and sat up straight and told him just as plain as she could speak, "Dr. Stansbury took my womanhood away." She announced, "He took it all out when I was seventeen. I can never have any children of my own."

Archie was shaken by this information. He felt an anger, too, and people say that when he came back to work after that day he was a changed man. But it hadn't changed his feelings for Beaula, he still wanted to marry her and in fact, they planned a wedding date. He was determined more than ever to get her out of the Stansbury house and make her his wife.

Beaula wanted to give Dr. Stansbury time to replace her, though, so she asked Archie to wait; they set the wedding date for one year later.

A month or so after the date was set Archie asked Beaula if there had been any applicants for her position in the Stansbury home.

Beaula again wrung her hands and avoided his gaze, "Not as of yet."

Archie trusted this woman, he would never have asked for her hand in marriage had he not, but he also knew she wasn't being exactly truthful. "What did the doc have to say about it when you told him?"

Beaula risked a glance at his face, but she wouldn't hold her eyes steady, "I didn't exactly tell him." Then she lifted her chin and thrust herself forward, placing her palms flat on Archie's chest, "It was the Missus I spoke to first about it. I had to tell her first. After all, she is the one who needs me the most, she is the one in such a weak condition, and she is the one who has to pick my replacement to help her care for that big house and the children still at home… it is her that I worry about the most!" It seemed after the words had tumbled from her lips there was no stopping her.

Archie securely draped an arm around her shoulder and they began to walk together as Beaula let it all out, or at least he thought it was all. Little did he know, she was barely scratching the surface, "It is the Missus who needs to be looked after. As for the children, they're easy compared to her, and with only two still at home almost grown, they aren't the ones who need me. She does.

"She may sound like a strong woman, but what you don't know is she has been ill. Only reason Mister wants her to answer the phones is to give her something to do and so he can keep an eye on her." Beaula seemed ashamed to be revealing the dirty little secrets she was sharing with Archie, but she trusted him. Besides, she needed to let it out. She had carried these secrets with her for so long and had never mentioned anything to anyone, no matter how many times she had been pumped to say something.

"She never has been the same since she lost those first two babies, and I don't mean she lost them, she gave birth to them. They were alive for a little while…. Or so she has said. I didn't come along 'til after the second one, you know?

"That's when the doctor realized she needed someone to help around the house. But she told me this, she told me she gave birth to those babies before their time and they were born gasping and writhing in pain, as they couldn't breathe for no more than a minute or so. She said the doctor told her after the second one she wasn't able to have children. The next time it might kill her. But he knew of ways to try and save her and maybe she could carry one… but she got such an infection, Archie, after that last baby."

Archie wished she wouldn't do this to herself as tears were spilling down her cheek. He didn't need to know these details, he only wanted to marry her and he wanted her to have a better life, "It's alright, Beaula…" he started.

But she interrupted finishing more of the details, "She never had any of their four children, Archie. She told me that herself. She said the doctor tried everything he could, but in the end the infection had scarred her womanly organs so badly, he had to take it all out. Kind of like what happened to me… only he said I had the same problem his wife did, it wasn't an infection for me. I was unable to carry a baby and he wanted to prevent me from going through what she had gone through."

"You've been pregnant before?" Archie softly inquired.

Beaula nodded, "By the doctor." It was almost a whispered confession, "He thought I might be able to have a baby for the Missus and she agreed, because she wanted a baby so much. After she had felt those first babies kicking inside of her and had made nurseries for two babies that never filled them…" Her voice trailed, and lifted again, "…she wanted her husband to father a child, so she consented to me carrying a baby… but then I started bleeding after a few months. Not as far as the Missus had carried hers, I never felt any movement." This is when

Beaula began to sob more raggedly, her bosom heaving as she thought back on it. Or maybe it was her thinking forward that brought so much pain.

Archie pulled her close, looking out over the world that surrounded them. The anger he had felt when she first told him about how and why she couldn't have children (thanks to Dr. Stansbury) had returned and at that moment he hated both of the rich Stansburys, because they were selfish people.

"But we didn't carry on no affair." She told Archie, looking deep into his eyes as he pulled back to view her, "It just happened a few times for the purpose of giving the Missus a baby, after that, he didn't come to my bed anymore."

"But he must have gone to someone's bed four more times, is that what you're telling me? Or they adopted them from an orphanage?" Somehow he knew the answer, somehow he knew they hadn't adopted. Not when the intent had been for the Mister to father children. "Those are **his** children? Not **hers**?"

Beaula nodded, "I suppose. I mean, I don't have any way of knowing who their Daddy is. When it got closer to the baby's arrival date, Mister would tell folks that Faye was confined to bed rest. For months nobody saw her, except me, of course. I knew the truth.

"Then, the doctor would bring a baby to her. It seemed to make her happy at first. I mean, she loved all the babies, she always showed love to the babies when she held them and she rocked them like a mother would, but I'd catch her sometimes, looking at them like she wondered things. Like maybe it hurt her somewhere deep, deep inside."

Archie was torn between his feelings of anger towards the Stansburys and his pity for their situation. He wanted to tell Beaula that he understood, but in reality, he didn't. "How did they talk you into it?"

Beaula lifted her chin and searched his eyes. Realizing he wasn't judging her, she shrugged, "I was young. I wouldn't agree to it now, I can tell you that. But I felt so sorry for the Missus, you can't know how much she cried and longed for those babies... But, I will always believe she was longing for the two of hers that died."

Beaula and Archie stood there in their own private area where they met and had carried on a courtship for several years, having picnics, sometimes dancing to a song that was only in their heads. On this day they held one another and they thought about their lives. They thought about how they wanted to be together. How far away it seemed, the reality of it. They thought about how much time they had already lost and how they didn't want to lose anymore.

After a long time Archie said, "You do want to marry me and come live with me, away from the Stansbury house, don't you?"

"More than anything." She whispered.

"Then how about I talk to the Stansburys?" He asked. Archie wouldn't let her know how much he wanted to say to them. In fact, he never did let her know his feelings regarding her employers.

"As long as you promise you won't tell them what I spoke of today." She put a finger to his lips before he could answer, "As long as you love me and forgive me for what I did. I sure don't want to start our marriage carrying all these secrets."

Archie's eye teared for a second as he thought about her worrying over him again, "I forgave you the minute you told me, "The way I see it, they have to answer for that, you was not more than a child yourself. They took advantage of you, took advantage of your caring nature and your willingness to give and think of others before yourself." He kissed her then. This kiss was unlike any they had ever shared, because it came from the depths of their hearts.

Archie decided then and there that Beaula had always given so much of herself to others, he would make certain he gave to her so that she could feel worthy, could forgive herself and enjoy life not always worrying about the Mister and Missus or the four Stansbury children.

Archie tried not to betray her trust when he spoke of the Stansburys to his closest friends. He shared some of the details on occasion, but he didn't always recognize how much he revealed.

Sometimes his anger would overcome him and he would rant and rave to Glenn, his neighbor, and once he even told him, "If I could, I'd wrap my hands around that doctor's neck and…" all the while he would demonstrate how he'd choke the man, never finishing his threat with words.

He knew he needed some time before he spoke to either Stansbury, time to calm down and plan things. Beaula had promised that she would speak more to Faye about their engagement and the need for them to hire a replacement, it seemed she liked Faye the best and could speak with her, but not so much the doctor.

The day finally came when he had to make the call.

When Faye Stansbury took the phone call, she didn't have a quiver in her voice. It was such a contrast to how he thought she would sound.

"Is this Mrs. Stansbury?" Archie inquired after the operator put the call through.

"It is, and who am I speaking with?" Her tone was professional and almost joyful. Beaula had said they knew how to behave around people. She had told him if no one knew any better they had the perfect life.

"This is Archie Moses." He wondered if she would recognize his name. Surely Beaula had mentioned him by name.

"Archie… Moses." She repeated, "I know that name, but Mr. Moses, I don't think you're a patient…" her voice trailed off, the first and only hint that she **did** know exactly who he was.

"I'm not a patient. I need to speak with the doctor, though, not on the phone, mind you. I need to meet with him, maybe meet with you both. Could you look at his schedule and find a time that would be good for all of us to talk? I'm engaged to Beaula, you know?"

If Faye Stansbury was a weak woman, she didn't sound it on the phone, "Yes, you are engaged to my dearest Beaula. Unfortunately, I don't see a time when the doctor could meet with you…"

"I understand." Archie kindly interrupted, "I can come there. It won't take very long. We can sit on the porch, I don't have to come inside. I feel it only proper to meet you

113

both and talk to you about the approaching wedding and Beaula's leave."

Faye could be heard rustling papers, "How about this Friday evening, then, Mr. Moses? Around dusk? Unless something unforeseen happens, I look forward to meeting you." She didn't wait for his answer, she simply wished him a good day and hung up.

It didn't sound like Faye Stansbury was all that frail, but he would make that opinion when they met. As far as Archie was concerned, it couldn't be too soon.

It was unusual for Beaula to meet with him in between their dates, they sometimes chatted when she came to buy groceries, but as far as it went he rarely saw her more often than on those occasions. So he was rather surprised when she showed up at the grocery store the next morning, "We need to speak." She told him and then moved away from the counter until he came around to her.

"Is there something wrong?"

"It's the Missus. She told me you're coming by the house Friday evening."

"Yes, to speak to them about our marriage and they need to find your replacement." Archie acknowledged.

"She didn't realize I would be leaving, Archie." Beaula stated, "She thought I would continue working there. They agreed to shorten my days so we could be together, but she didn't think I'd ever leave. She's took to her bed, she is sick, Archie!"

He didn't know what to say. He was stunned. A few of the workers noticed that he seemed to swell up like a mad bull frog. "You don't want me to talk to Dr. Stansbury?"

"Of course I do, but now, with this... what will we do?"

"Beaula, this is a little thing, replacing a housekeeper." Archie fired, "That insane ole woman has depended on you for too much. She can't expect you to just stay with them 'til the day you die."

Beaula placed a calming hand on his arm, "Will you promise me you'll be careful of your words with them? Will you promise me if they don't agree to let me go, you'll accept it? If they don't agree we can elope. Will you promise me that, Archie?"

He searched her eyes, her big trusting eyes. He saw the love she felt for him, but he also saw something else. A look he didn't understand or have a name for. But he loved her, and he knew she would elope with him if it came to that. He simply didn't understand what was going on right now. How could he not agree, though? "Of course," He sighed, and turned away, returning to his position behind the counter. "I guess I will see you Friday."

Beaula didn't answer. He looked up to see her back as she walked away. It appeared she was crying.

This didn't dampen his anger towards her employers, in fact, it added fuel. Archie did something very uncharacteristic of his ways that day, he cursed out loud in front of a customer and two store employees.

When Friday evening came Archie wasn't in the best of moods, he had fretted and lost sleep the night before. In his dreams he vividly saw himself killing Dr. Stansbury, that's why he hadn't slept well. He knew it was just his anger and he trusted himself to go there, but he was afraid he wouldn't be able to keep his promise to Beaula, that he wouldn't be able to watch his words.

You see, he had never met the doctor. Sure, he had seen him out in town and different places, but Archie was a healthy man, and except for the occasional cold he didn't need to see a doctor.

From what he could remember the doctor seemed to be a mild mannered person. He hoped this was the case on this day, because in spite of the promise he had made to his lovely fiancé, he wasn't exactly sure he could mind his tongue.

When he approached the front of the house he was in awe of the beauty of the home. Archie was a simple man, and he wasn't impressed with material things, but he did have a sinking feeling in the pit of his stomach that maybe Beaula wouldn't be happy living in his humble home. How could she, coming from a stately structure such as this?

He heard someone clear their throat, which startled him momentarily and he turned on heel to see the doctor coming up from the basement entrance. The graying man had turned the closed sign on the door and was carrying the keys to his office.

"Hello, Dr. Stansbury, I am Archie Moses." He extended his hand as the elder man approached.

Still of straight stature, the doctor stood eye to eye with Archie. His hair was thinning on top and gray had replaced a lot of the brown.

Dr. Stansbury looked at Archie's hand, "Would you take that back? I might have germs, need to wash up. I treated a man for the syph a little while ago and even though I've washed my hands, I won't feel any better about it until I've scrubbed them in hot water and alcohol." He dipped his hands inside his trouser pockets, depositing the keys there, but not withdrawing them, "Glad to meet you, though."

Archie wasn't sure how to reply to that. He was at once flooded with so many thoughts it was all he could do to fall in stride behind the man and follow him to the

117

porch. Finally he inquired, "Are we going inside? I would prefer we leave Beaula out of this."

"Me, too, and for that matter I wish you had left Faye out of it." The doctor whirled around. "She is a sick woman, Mr. Moses, and she can't take too much stress over things like this. I realize you probably didn't know that. But right now she is most weak."

Archie felt his resentment start to rise so he immediately found himself a seat in a rocker and dropped his weight into it, taking in a deep breath of air, "I'm sorry to hear that, I didn't realize this about your wife. I am trying to do the right thing, though and make certain you're aware that Beaula will be my wife in half a year and I will want her to come to my house and live."

"That's to be respected, son, but we have already worked it out. Beaula can work three or four days a week here and then come home to you on the remaining days."

Archie looked at the man who was standing on the porch, both men studying one another. Archie pondered why it was so hard for the doctor to let Beaula go. "Beaula says she has been with you most of her life. I reckon she's like a daughter to you." It was hard to say that aloud as any decent man wouldn't have intimate relations with his daughter.

Stansbury sat down in the swing then, many feet away, but still within good earshot, "She is like family in many ways. I have entrusted Beaula to my family for many, many years." He seemed to let his gaze go distant and his eyes seemed unfocused as he told Archie, "But it is my wife who is my concern."

"Beaula mentioned that Faye relied on her quite a bit." Archie stated. How could he make this man understand that Beaula would not be working there after their marriage? "I guess it is none of my business how you run yours, but can't you find someone else who can come into your family much the way Beaula did…" his words trailed off, because he sure didn't want anyone to be in that situation, "someone you and your wife could trust and could hire to replace Beaula?"

The doctor eyed him suspiciously. Was he wondering how much Archie knew already? It was almost impossible to tell where his thoughts were. His eyes twitched nervously, but he regained his composure quickly and fired back, "And I didn't think it would make it this far."

"What's that, sir?"

The older man chuckled, "You and Beaula. I know you've been courting her for years. How many men could wait years, Mr. Moses, for one woman's hand and heart?"

Archie was dumbfounded.

"How many men WOULD wait?" The elder male challenged.

What, exactly, was this man talking about? Archie wasn't inclined to answer just yet, because by now he was clenching his fingers around the chair arm. He didn't trust himself to speak.

The doctor must have felt he had the younger fellow in a quandary, "You've been married before, Mr. Moses?" He inquired all too smugly.

"No sir. I was in the military a long while, though I've had a few love interests I haven't been married. I wanted to know in my heart that my wife would be with me until death. I believe I have found that in Beaula."

Again the doctor chuckled without humor, "I believe you have. But maybe there is something you don't know."

Archie braced himself for an unexpected admission from the doctor. He hadn't anticipated this.

"You see, I am also Beaula's doctor. She can't have any children, Mr. Moses. She is barren. And I might as well warn you, a barren woman becomes a crazy woman."

Archie stiffened, his fingers curling around the chair so tight his knuckles pinched white. He pictured Beaula's face and recalled her plea with him not to reveal the secrets she had shared, "Is that so, Doctor?"

The doctor nodded, "Might not should have told you that. But a man wants a son. All men want children to carry on the family name, Mr. Moses. That's why I figured I'd never have to worry about Beaula getting married. Not only that, how could a man fall in love with her? She is so hard to get to know."

Archie leaned forward in his rocker just then, his eyes narrowing and his lips thinning. For a moment he saw the doctor pull back in the swing and he saw those beady eyes twitch uncontrollably. If the doctor could have known the thoughts raging through Archie he wouldn't have been so brave.

It was perfect timing, because the front door eased open and there stood Beaula, her eyes darting between both men. "Mister," She spoke to the doctor, "The Missus is calling for you."

"Did you administer the cocktail, Beaula?"

"She wouldn't take it, not this time." Beaula said, nervously.

"What?" The doctor arose to his feet.

"Not this time. She insists on speaking with you." Beaula darted her eyes back to Archie.

The doctor seemed to waver in his spot, "Mr. Moses, I am glad you had the decency to approach me about your upcoming marriage to my dear servant, Beaula, and I do hope if you marry her in six months that you spend the rest of your lives as blessed as Faye and I have been."

There was something about that blessing that sent shivers up Beaula's spine and it had the same effect on Archie.

"So we've reached an agreement?" Archie dared ask.

The doctor didn't blink this time and he didn't move a muscle. "The agreement is between you and Beaula. I have a sick wife, so excuse me." He looked at Beaula who instinctively cleared the doorway for him.

Archie stood, then approached Beaula, waiting until he could no longer hear the doctor's footsteps before wrapping her in his arms.

She fell against him, sobbing.

"It's alright." He assured her, "We didn't have an argument. I am not sure if an agreement was reached…" he let his words trail.

"I love you, Archie." Was all she said.

In the ensuing months that followed, Faye never recovered well enough to answer the phones again and it seemed the doctor was declining, too. Beaula would confide in Archie that he seemed to be losing weight and had little or no appetite. She also confided that he seemed to be losing his mind. More than once she had seen him talking and mumbling to himself, or to someone who wasn't even there.

"I don't understand, Beaula, all this over losing their servant?" He even wondered if the doctor himself loved Beaula? "You sure he doesn't have feelings for you?"

"Archie," Beaula scolded, "I've already told you." She looked at him earnestly, "There is something awful going on inside them, Archie. I don't want our marriage to be like theirs." She paused, "The day he gave us his blessings, I feel he may have cursed us instead."

"Aww, that is impossible." Archie scoffed.

"Something is eating away at them both. It can't be all about me. But I seem to have started this." Guilt salted her words and weighed heavily on her shoulders.

Archie felt at once responsible. "I'm sorry, Beaula." He apologized and for a moment he thought that maybe they should postpone their wedding.

Beaula must have sensed that he was taking it the wrong way, "Why should you be sorry?" She asked, "You have given me the best moments of my life as we got to know one another atop our little mountain here." She spread her arms out and waved at their surroundings, "You always enjoy these moments, it's always enough just to spend our days together. You never ask for anything more, you always wait patiently for our time together." Her eyes were wide and glistening, "You are my love, Archie Moses. My true love."

He knew there were more words to follow, but he never expected how they would change his life, "Let's get married right away." She anxiously said, "Let's run away tonight!"

Archie was speechless, but he found a way to show Beaula his approval. He hoisted her up in his arms and twirled with her, laughing, the both of them until they almost cried.

They agreed Beaula would sneak out at midnight. It would be an hour after Faye would take her "cocktail", as the doctor described it. This was a mixture of several pills and some tonic he had prescribed years ago to calm her nerves.

The one she took at night was even more potent than the day time prescription. Within an hour of taking that one, a gunshot couldn't awaken Faye from sleep.

Beaula was nervous about disturbing Dr. Stansbury, though, he was a light sleeper. But if Beaula was quiet and walked slowly, maybe she wouldn't wake him.

It was agreed that Archie would wait for her at the end of the road and she would only take a few personal items and some clothing, which she would hide in a sack at the stream behind the house, not too far from the cemetery.

Beaula had already placed it there, it was the first thing she did when she returned to the house after the meeting with Archie.

She was startled by Faye when she returned from hiding the sack of clothing and a few scant belongings she couldn't part with.

"Beaula, there you are." The woman's speech was slurred, as it often was these days. She was standing on the sidewalk not too many steps from the porch, "I have been looking all over for you."

"Why, it's Sunday, Missus, remember?" Beaula's voice was unsteady and she detected it. Hopefully the Missus didn't sense anything out of the ordinary.

It wasn't uncommon for Faye to get her days of the week mixed up. Her life consisted of bathing, sleeping, nibbling on food and roaming the hallways. Sometimes she could be found writing in her diary. She had always enjoyed writing in a journal. But lately, she seemed to write less often.

Faye's eyes were heavy and the pupils dilated, "Sunday? Then where is that husband of mine?" She looked aimlessly out over the yards. "I've called for everyone, not a soul will answer. I guess the children are ignoring me."

"Missus, the children are away at church, all day services and gathering to eat afterwards." Beaula reminded, relaxing a bit. Surely Faye would not sense that something was amiss.

On most Sundays Beaula didn't return home until dark. She spent every minute of daylight with Archie on those days when she could, never rushing home.

"Then Clyde is dining with someone." Accused Faye shrilly. "We both know he wouldn't entertain himself with the children, now would he?"

Lately Faye had been very belligerent with her husband. It seemed she didn't hesitate to tell him what she thought and in honesty, she wasn't telling any lies.

Beaula forced a dry chuckle, "No, Missus, we both know that."

Again, the Stansbury family may have had most people fooled, as they were very cordial to one another, but there wasn't a lot of affection to spread around.

"Do you reckon it's that new nurse, Patty the batty?" Asked Faye, laughing like a young school girl.

Beaula didn't realize he had a new nurse. In fact, the nurses who currently worked there were married with families of their own. But sometimes Faye was known to regress in the past.

"He may be eating at a church picnic with the whole congregation instead." Beaula offered.

"Pooh!" Faye waved , turning away as they walked towards the house, "He may have you fooled, Beaula, but he hasn't fooled me with his dalliances. He hasn't fooled himself, either! I see him wandering around in the cemetery, feeling guilty for the lives he didn't save. Feeling guilty for the lives he may have cost. I see him going to church on Sundays in hopes of saving his soul from the pits of hell, when he never spent a day in a church house until lately! You can't tell me Clyde Stansbury ever believed in God until recently, Beaula! Not that man! He thought **he was** God, thought he could take a life in the name of medical science, thought he could save a life when death was on the front doorsteps of one of his patients, save them with his medical education and his superior knowledge! Not that man! HE can't even save his own family. HE can't even save his own soul!"

The words cut through Beaula as it seemed there was some delight sprinkled in with the hatred that spewed from Faye's mouth. "Missus, would you like a drink? Would you like to lie down?"

Faye stopped walking, as they were now in the kitchen, "Drink?" She repeated and for a moment it seemed she contemplated it, "You and Clyde always think I need something to drink. What do you think I am, a drunkard?" Her words were vile and her stare heated.

Faye had never looked at Beaula this way before. "I'm sorry, Missus, I didn't mean any disrespect."

"No, of course you didn't." Faye spat, in a mocking tone, "He has you fooled, too, doesn't he?" Her eyes were darting across Beaula's face, "No, I don't need a drink, maybe you should pour yourself one!" She started to stomp away, her heels clicking quickly on the floor. Then she paused, "Oh, Beaula, do you know the reason I was calling your name?"

Beaula answered, "No, ma-am."

"Because I thought I heard someone in the house with me. But how could that be? It's Sunday, isn't it, Beaula? And no one is ever home on Sundays." Faye strolled away. Leaving a cold bitter air hanging thickly in the kitchen, Beaula shivered.

Had Faye heard her packing and carrying her sack of a few possessions out of the house? Obviously she had heard something. But Beaula didn't ponder it anymore. After tonight, she and Archie would be free.

At eleven pm when she took Faye the "cocktail". She found the Missus sitting in bed, writing in her diary. "Your nightly cocktail, Missus." She approached cautiously, as Faye eyed her from her position on the bed.

"Put it on my night stand, Beaula" Faye instructed. Her voice softer than her stare, softer than it had been earlier. "I want to finish this final thought before I retire."

"Yes, ma-am." Beaula acknowledged as she put the tray on the nightstand.

"I hope I didn't offend you earlier." Faye uttered as she scribbled in the diary.

Beaula couldn't exactly lie, "I am sorry I upset you. I may have deserved it." Was all she could say.

"You didn't deserve such a rude outburst." Faye told her, "You have always been very loyal, more so than even my own husband and children." She looked at Beaula then, "I ask for your forgiveness."

"You are forgiven." Beaula almost bent to hug her, but Faye put her finger in the air.

"I hope that everyone I have ever hurt will forgive me as well. Even your fellow Mr. Archie Moses, for my being so greedy of you." Faye stopped writing and studied Beaula at length, "You will pass along my apology, won't you? You will tell him? In case we never meet."

Her words alarmed Beaula, who stumbled as she stepped backwards, looking accusingly down at the floor at the throw rug crumpled beneath her feet. Searching for an answer she kneeled to straighten the rug, her hands atremble as she was most nervous, "I appreciate your concern, Missus." She said, pulling at the rug. "I must go now, have a pleasant sleep."

Beaula turned and she could feel Faye's eyes at her backside. She worried that Faye sensed something out of the ordinary. The oddity was so thick in the room it nearly stifled Beaula. She was very relieved to exit the room and close the door between her and the woman she had known longer than even a family member.

She glanced at the clock as she passed it on her way back to her room, it seemed time was ticking by so slowly. Her heart was aflutter, yet she had to be calm and wait until she could leave, until she could meet with Archie.

She also checked her reflection in the mirror as she passed. She most definitely looked guiltily nervous, her large eyes wider than normal, her mouth pulled into a tight grimace. Beaula sucked in deep, cleansing air and patted the loose hairs that had fallen from her braid.

Inside her room she smoothed over the bed covers, made certain the window curtains were neat, adjusted a porcelain figure on a shelf and sighed.

She looked around at her room. She would be glad to be free from it all. Though she had a most beautiful house to care for, children that had always been dear to her, she would be so happy to never return to the fortress of the Stansbury home.

She had packed a picture of the four children in her sack, she didn't want to forget them. They were good people, those four who were innocent of the lies and secrets that shamed their parents.

She knew the Stansburys could afford to hire a wonderful servant. Maybe a clean slate would be good for the Mister and Missus, that way the secrets could stay in their closets where they probably belonged.

Beaula again checked the clock. She knew Archie was very near his appointed destination, she could almost count on it.

By now Faye would be fast asleep. As for the Mister, well, she hoped he was in bed, too. She would have to take her chances.

If she failed, she could make an excuse and return to her room and wait for a second chance. She firmly believed in second chances.

Beaula's palms were sweaty when she opened her bedroom door. She peered out; of course there wasn't much to see except the stairs down to the main level living.

She eased the door closed behind her which made the narrow passage much too dark for her eyes to adjust quickly. But her eyes did adjust and she stepped slowly and deliberately down each landing until she was on the polished marble that was the library's flooring.

Now her eyes were well adjusted and moonlight was spilling in through the windows here and there.

Beaula took deliberate, easy steps. Quiet steps, she hoped. She tried not to breathe too loud, either, but that was the sound she heard, her own breathing. Surely that sound could wake no one. She was simply nervous, that's all.

Tip toeing through the kitchen, she wondered if she should exit through that door or the main door. It occurred to her she hadn't planned everything through.

The kitchen was farther away from the bedrooms, but was also farther from the stream where her sack awaited her. Well, once outside she took less risk of being found. So she eased open the kitchen door and slipped outside.

The night was bright with not a cloud in the sky. In fact, the sky was almost purple with glimmers of lights from the stars. This would be a perfect night to slip away with Archie. Her heart was pounding hard behind her breast.

The grass was wet and she could already feel the dampness penetrating her shoes as she hurried away from the house, approaching the cemetery in the near distance. She could see the big oak tree and a few of the shadowy shapes from headstones beneath the tree. She didn't like the cemetery, but the stream was just beyond it and that was the last thing that attached her to the house. Once she had the sack, she would be on her way to Archie, on her way to a new life. She knew it must be a few minutes after midnight, she had better pick up her pace.

Beaula never once looked behind her, she never stole a glance back at the house. Even if she had, even if she dared look back and saw that she had been spotted she was not returning to the house now. It was destined in her heart; she would be with the man she loved.

She walked past the graveyard, slowing her stride and was very close to the stream now. She could smell the freshness of the water and hear the pleasant movement of water over the rocks. She strained her eyes, searching for her sack. She remembered the general location, but it was difficult at best to even locate a shape similar to it. If she just patiently walked where she thought it might be…

"Looking for this?"

Beaula froze. Her heart seemed to miss a beat and she turned toward the familiar voice.

Clyde Stansbury stood less than twenty feet away and he was holding her sack. "This is yours, isn't it Beaula?"

"Yes sir." She was surprised how strong her voice sounded. Inside she was shaking hard.

"Where do you think you're going?" His voice actually was shakier than hers. Lately, it had become raspier, too, but these would not be her thoughts this night.

"Is that any business of yours, Mister?" Beaula was contemplating what to do, "Maybe I am meeting my lover. Maybe we do that sometimes."

"The things in this sack suggest something else." Dr. Stansbury said, "Looks to me like you're running away!"

"No sir." Beaula said and decided that maybe she could do without the sack. She started backing away. She knew she could out run him.

"Beaula, do you know what you've done to my family?" He took a step towards her, "Do you know how you have wrecked my home?"

Beaula didn't answer. She took a few more steps away, but he took even more steps, bringing him closer.

She turned then, her foot slipping in the wet grass. She caught her balance and started to run.

"Won't do you any good!" He called out.

Beaula didn't risk stopping or worrying about his threat. She was younger and in better health than he was, all she had to do was keep running.

She actually felt the bullet hit her before she heard the sound slicing rancid through the perfect night air. Was it her voice that cried out "NO!" when she fell to the ground, gripping her bloody wet side?

She turned her face and looked at him. He was holding a pistol, rapidly approaching her.

"I thought you were a burglar." Dr. Stansbury said potently, "I couldn't tell who you were." His voice was evil and she knew he was plotting his alibi, "Why, everyone knows I have a lot of money and a robber wouldn't be too farfetched."

Beaula could feel intense heat spreading from her side, dispersing rapidly throughout her body and she wanted at once to fall back on the wet grass, the cool wet grass. But she also knew he was going to pump another bullet into her because he still held the gun with his outstretched arm, "You will never get away with this." She told him and started to crawl away, trying to rise to her feet again.

"Oh won't I?" He jeered, "I will, Beaula, and you know what else? I already have a grave to put you in."

"Unless you fill it first!" A woman's voice screamed and both Beaula and Clyde looked to see Faye Stansbury standing in her night robe, not fifteen feet away, "I saw you shoot her, Clyde! I saw you! Are you going to shoot me now?" Her voice was so shrill and she was holding something. Her hand was quivering but it appeared she was holding a gun.

Beaula kept crawling away, she had never stopped inching away. She watched Faye, she saw her point the gun at Clyde.

When the shot rang out Beaula didn't flinch as her hearing was congested now, and her eyes were unfocused. Faye's words weren't making any sense. Words about finding Clyde gone from his bed, about knowing he'd be in the graveyard. How the gun cabinet was open and so she picked up the little 22 pistol.

Beaula didn't even realize that the words did make sense, they were coming to her in fragments and bits and pieces… making no connections….and she was getting so cold. The heat that had previously burned inside now drained out of her in thin rivulets of blood, being replaced by such deeply penetrating cold… and her lips were so numb now… so numb….

Beaula thought she was getting away, she was determined and when she heard Archie's voice she thought she had actually crawled to him. "Archie," She weakly called out, opening her eyes for the sight of him.

"Beaula!" He called out and she heard his loud footsteps, "You shot her!" He screamed, "You killed her!"

"Not yet." Came a weaker male voice not too far away, "Not yet." This was the voice from the doctor.

"Put that gun down!" A woman's voice screamed. It was Faye's voice.

Shots rang out again before an eerie calm fell upon the night.

When the children had heard the gun shots, they both went in search of their parents. When they didn't find their parents, they had gone up to Beaula's room. Of course they were frightened to find no one there, so they returned to hide in their parent's bedroom until there were no more gun shots. Then they heard their mother's voice, and she was coming into the room!

"Mother!" They had both called out, running to her.

They saw that Faye's eyes were wide, almost bugging out of her head and she was smiling, too, this wide, stiff smile. "Children!" She opened her arms and encircled them both, "It's alright." She said in a sing-song voice.

"We heard gun shots."

"Father thought there was a burglar." She told her children in rushed words."But everything is alright now." She ushered them towards their rooms, "Everything is alright."

"Where's Father?"

"He'll be home." She said, "He'll be home soon, after he's made sure there is no burglar," all the while Faye wore that spooked look on her face, "Mother has to take her medicine now." She told the younger folk, "You know how I need my medicine. Now go on, everything is going to be alright."

It wasn't until early morning that the tragedy unfolded. The children were awakened by police officers, illumination from the flash lights traveling through the windows in the wee morning hours. Monotone voices could be heard resonating in the large house as the officers conducted their business.

There had been reports of gun fire and after searching the grounds the officers discovered one body outside, that of the doctor, near the cemetery; and one body inside, this was the mother. Thankfully, the children were unharmed.

The father had died from multiple gunshot wounds. The mother from a suicide cocktail of pills and tonic; later a message in her journal would be found with a message of apology to her children.

That morning after day break the officers had followed a blood trail from the cemetery through the woods and at times lost the trail of blood, but could still follow broken limbs on saplings and boot marks in the dampened parts of the woods. They found the other two bodies atop the lookout.

The couple appeared to be sharing one last look over the bluff, as that is how they were found; the female lying over the male's chest and lap and he with his arm protectively thrown across her. She had been shot in the side, the bullet exiting her body in back. She had obviously bled to death.

As for the man… as for Archie Moses, it appeared he had carried Beaula to their old courting grounds. It appeared as though he had taken the same small 22 caliber pistol that had fired all but one bullet into the doctor. That one remaining bullet had been fired into Archie's temple, obviously self inflicted.

To this day, there is much mystery still surrounding the legacy that was the Stansbury household. Speculations as to who killed whom, and why the murders and suicides transpired raged wild among those who knew the foursome. Rumors are like diseases spreading quickly and growing stronger.

In the many years the house has stood atop the grassy knoll many owners have come and gone. But they all share similar stories.

There is a lady that roams the halls in a night robe, her heels clicking on the marble floors, her apparition fading away into the master bedroom.

In the basement, the stench of medicine and sometimes illness, similar to the smell in most all clinics permeates the room. On occasion people have heard the sounds of a weak infant's cry echo through the walls.

Then there is the smell that comes on the anniversary of the tragedy. Every year, especially when the moon is bright, screams can be heard on the wind and the nauseating, rich aroma of blood fills the air in and around the stony house. A rich smell that lingers in the nostrils and in the throats of the unfortunate occupants.

In the cemetery, on certain nights a shadowy figure paces back and forth. Sometimes the same shadowy figure will visit the basement, disappearing through one of the walls, the sound of keys on a ring jingling a solemn tone.

But the one vision that even the towns people can count on, if you go there on the anniversary of the murders and suicide, is that of a saddened figure of a lone man carrying his loved one to the top of their favorite lookout and gingerly sitting down with her before the sound of a gunshot echoes from the mountain top.

The End

A Word from the Author:

This book has been dedicated to my family and friends and to anyone reading it who loves ghost stories, folklore, and urban legends.

The art of telling spooky tales around a campfire is a dwindling affair. That's really too bad as generations will miss the spirit of such a gathering (pun intended).

I have many more eerie tales of specters and superstitions and supernatural events.

Please enjoy the excerpt of the following story set in Anderson County, TN., which will be published in an upcoming book.

It, too, is based on a true experience. Already the story has been repeated to several generations.

An Excerpt from The Devil at Grandma's

I had been taught my entire life that the devil comes in many disguises. That the devil, the one mentioned in the Bible who is also known as Lucifer, yes that one. THE devil can be handsome, clever, charming and beguiling.

Of course, I never thought I would meet him. I figured he was a spirit at best; a negative feeling; or a little voice inside our head; or the temptation in our heart that leads us astray. Or maybe a snake, like the one mentioned in the Bible that appeared to Eve in the Garden of Eden.

Never did I think that the devil would be an unassuming person like you or me, not until I came face to face with him.

Maybe you will say that he wasn't the devil; maybe you will say that he wasn't even real. But I have the scars to prove it. If you don't believe me, maybe you should read my story.

When I was thirteen my parents, my brother and I moved to Tennessee to be near my paternal grandmother Rose.

She was getting older, having health problems, and Dad was her only son.

We didn't live too far away to begin with, just the other side of the Kentucky line. I still don't understand why we had to be uprooted from our happy home, since we had room for Grandma to come live with us in Kentucky, but I didn't have any say so in the matter.

Besides, Grandma could be stubborn, she didn't want to move.

After Grandpa died, Grandma Rose called us often. A few times she visited for a weekend, but she hated leaving her home, and she always made Dad feel guilty for not visiting more than he did.

I understood why Dad didn't want to visit her, after all, walking into Grandma's house was like walking into a shrine for Grandpa. She wouldn't let anyone sit in his recliner, his house-slippers were beside the bed, and she had a place at the table set just for him. Even though we all knew Grandpa wasn't coming back, I think Grandma hoped he would.

About the Author:

Tammy J. Poore lives in East Tennessee with her husband, two children, and a multitude of pets.

She has always loved a ghost story. As a child she enjoyed frightening friends with scary tales.

She has been writing most of her life, enjoying a job as a newspaper correspondent for a local paper in the mid to late1980's. After that she pursued two other careers and was successful with each endeavor.

However, a paranormal experience in 2009 rekindled her lust for chasing ghost stories, thrusting her back into writing about the mysterious and elusive spirits that quiet possibly live alongside us.

Tammy resided in an actual "haunted" house in her teenage years and has had many "mysterious" encounters. There was an extended absence of "eerie" events, until the night she stayed in a haunted hotel....Now she spends her free time chasing local ghost stories and has devoted a website to chronicle the experiences.

www.ingramcontent.com/pod-product-compliance
Lightning Source LLC
Chambersburg PA
CBHW060430130626
46555CB00005B/2297